MOUNT ZION PLAYS

*WAITING FOR THE PRINCE

TRIBULATION NIGHT

(With Poetic Embrace of "Tribulation Night"
by: Olumide Oki)

Mike Bamiloye

Introduction

For many years, the Mount Zion Faith Ministries Int'l, Nigeria, went about many churches and campuses in various towns and cities of Nigeria presenting an allegorical drama depicting the spiritual condition of the church of God, the compromising stand of many believers of this time and the manifestation of the spirit of impatience in the life of many Christians of today. The drama hammered on the significance of preparing for the second coming of the Lord Jesus Christ. That drama was titled: "The Return of the Bridegroom". The Live Performance was first staged in the year 1989.

In 1991, the drama was made into the ministry's second major movie: "The Last Generation" which was later re-edited and re-titled "The Bride and the Devil". The drama was adjusted and presented as musical drama under another title: "The King Is Coming" in 1999.

Now, the evergreen message is presented again with a more appropriate title and shot into a beautiful and colorful movie by Mount Zion Film Productions, Nigeria, in conjunction with the Flaming Sword Film Ministries, Dallas, Texas, and titled: "WAITING FOR THE PRINCE".

It is a message of urgency and necessity for all who desire to make it to Heaven at last.

Between 1982 and 1983, Evang. Mike Bamiloye had written and produced "Like A Thief in the Night" for the Christian Fellowship Drama Unit of the College of Education, Ilesha, Osun State, Nigeria. The drama was staged by the Drama Unit of the fellowship on the campus and in many places, while he was a student on the campus.

In 1990, the Mount Zion Faith Ministries came up with a more detailed version of the drama. The drama presentation is based on the aftermath of the Rapture; the agonies and tortures of the believers who would miss the sudden disappearance of all true believers all over the world. It was a full-length drama that was only staged about two or three times before the ministry decided to make the drama the first major movie.

Thus, in the later part of 1990, the Mount Zion Faith Ministries made the first major movie titled: "The Beginning of the End" The first few copies of the movie were sent to ministers of God to show to their church members and workers. The movie had a massive effect on the lives of many people and the movie was used for crusades and revivals by many churches.

Because of the relevance of the end-time message in the movie to the present spiritual and physical conditions of the church and the world, the ministry found it very necessary to present adaptations of the movie on stage on many occasions under the titles: "Any Moment from Now" and a shorter version of the drama titled: "A Dream of Rapture".

By the leading of the Lord, in 2010, the author re-wrote the script in a more detailed form and the ministry decided to shoot this evergreen message of the end-time with modern equipment exhibition of the presently available technology. The new script was shot again with the title:" Tribulation Night"

I strongly believe that the two soul-searching and thought-provoking dramas will prepare your heart for the soon coming

of our Dear Savior Jesus Christ.   Remain Blessed.
MIKE BAMILOYE.
December 2013.
Reprint: October 2023

Characters:

ANITA

PRINCE

SHALOM

PASTOR

VICTORIA

NELSON

LARRY

SITANDA

HILARY

EUNICE

SIMEON

4 MALE SERVANTS

2 POLICEMEN

3 NEIGHBOURS

SCENE ONE:

(It is evening, somewhere in Garland, Texas, USA, inside the bedroom of a large house. A young lady sleeps on the bed; the large bedcover pulled over above her chest. A man, in singlet and casual trousers, sleeps on the bed beside her. The lady stirs awake, looks around sleepily, and then looks at her wristwatch. Then, she rises and begins to wake up the young man beside her.)

ANITA: Please, wake up...! Wake up...! My God...! It is 10:30 already. *(Larry stirs awake, trying to focus his eyes.)*

LARRY: I thought you said you would stay over tonight and go back home early tomorrow morning.

ANITA: *(hurriedly)* I never promised you that, Sweetie.

LARRY: *(pulling her hand)* Come on, Baby. Last week you slept over just once, but you have said you will make it twice this week, so, why can't you sleep over tonight.?

ANITA: Not tonight, probably on Thursday or Friday....no not Friday...my Pastor will notice my absence in the Friday night vigil...Maybe Saturday night. *(She dashes to the dressing mirror and begins to brush, fixing her hair and powdering her face. The young man rises from the bed and goes into the restroom. Her phone rings and she quickly brings it out from her bag, and puts it on:*

ANITA: Hello...! Who is this? Who...? Ah...Simeon...Simeon...How is it? How far?
(Nigeria. It is afternoon. A young man in a shirt and tie comes out of an office room, inside a large office building somewhere in Lagos. He is on the phone talking impatiently.)

SIMEON: Just coming back from the Embassy. The same old story. And that will be the fourth time I would be turned back at the Embassy. They simply refused to give me the Visa upon all the overwhelming documents. I think I am getting fed up with the whole thing.

ANITA: No, Honey, don't lose your faith. Don't be discouraged so easily. *(Her man-friend is trying to hurry her up, but she is calming him down while talking on the phone.)*

SIMEON: That is not the issue, Anita. The issue is, that you have been there in the US now for almost two years and that was just two months after our wedding. We were still believing the Lord for a child when you got a Visa to come over there, while my

papers were being processed. We all thought I would join you within two or three months, but this is the second year.
(The man-friend is showing signs of impatience again. She calms him down roughly, whispering to him)

ANITA: *(covers the phone mouthpiece and whispers quickly to the man in a hushed tone)* What is wrong with you?... I am talking to my husband...! *(she continues talking to her husband on the phone)* Simeon, I know you are trying...but try more. You can still re-apply for the Visa or...

SIMEON: *(anxiously)* Listen to me, Sweet-Heart, are we not married to stay together? Why should we be married and still be living like a widow and a widower? Is that the plan of God for us?

ANITA: So, what else do you want me to do now?

SIMEON: This is almost two years. When are we going to start building our home? If I can't come over there, then, for the sake of our marriage, for the sake of our blessed union and the home the Lord promised to give us, come back home, and let's be together. That is the will of God.

ANITA: I can't. My papers are not yet complete, I can't travel yet.

SIMEON: *(dejected)* So, when will your papers be complete?

ANITA: I am still working on it. Hopefully, in the next five or six months.

SIMEON: That was what you said last year.

ANITA: I am sure it shall be possible this year.

SIMEON: Alright...How is everything?

ANITA: I am managing...things are not easy.

SIMEON: I know...I know...not for me either. I am trying to hold on. It is not easy...My colleagues here in the office always make jest of me...they call me a Married Bachelor...It's not easy.

ANITA: I am sorry...Honey. I know we shall be together soon.

SIMEON: Where are you now?

ANITA: Front of the church. We just finished the Gospel Service, and I am going home.

SIMEON: We are in a 7-day prayer and fasting in the church. We are rounding up this evening...I have prayed and fasted on today's Visa interview, but I was turned down all the same...the Lord understands. How is your uncle?

ANITA: He is always talking about you. We are praying for you here too. (*The man is pulling her again, and becoming more impatience*) Honey, I've got to go. I

you now?
ANITA: I am presently in my room sir. I have decided to take some time to rest. I am resting at home, sir.

PASTOR: (*smiles wryly*) Alright, Vicky

ANITA: Thank you, Pastor. I am very grateful. *(Turning to Larry guiltily)* that is my Pastor.
*(Larry pulls out of the parking lot and drives out to the crawling traffic on the highway.)*3

will call you back later…

SIMEON: (*reluctantly*) Alright…I will be expecting…

ANITA: Bye. (*Conversation over. She turns sharply to the man*) Larry, What…? What's your problem? I was talking with my husband…and you can't even show a little courtesy for being with his wife.

LARRY: (*jovially*) Baby, who gives a damn about a man who is thousands of miles away? How are you sure he is not sorting himself out the way you are doing here?

ANITA: (*guiltily*) No, I trust him.

LARRY: (*sneeringly*) Yeah, just as he trusts you too…. (*Anita looks away shamefully*) look here, my dear, I have a wife at home too, but there is nothing like being with a dearly loving person like you. So, be happy at what makes you happy, Baby.
(*Next, we see them walking out of the house, holding hands, to the drive outside where the car is. They enter the car, and her phone rings again, she quickly brings out the phone from inside her bag. She looks at the caller and freezes a bit.*)

ANITA: Hello…Daddy, Pastor…. Evening sir. …Yes, sir, I couldn't come to the church this evening because of the load of work I had to encounter in the office today. I worked till around eight this evening.

PASTOR: (*sitting on a couch in a living room*) So where are

SCENE TWO

(She arrives at the front of the house. The man drops her, and she walks to the door, opens the door, and enters. She closes the door behind her and turns the key; she freezes in shock as she stares at an elderly man sitting on the couch with a Bible on his lap.)

ANITA: *(freezes with fear)* Daddy…!

PASTOR: *(with a low emotional tone)* I scared you?

ANITA: *(tries to calm herself).* Yes,

PASTOR: I am very sorry to burst into your house unannounced. I have tried my best to get your attention, including calling your number without a response. I sent your friend to you to see me in my office, but you refused to come.

ANITA: *(still in shock).* How did you….?

PASTOR: Eunice, your friend opened the door for me. I told her I needed to see you urgently. So, after the Bible

Studies, I came home with her. I got here; I didn't see you. So, I called you just to tell you I am around. But I was amazed when you told me on the phone that you are in your room, resting after a hectic day. That is a confirmation of what the Lord told me about you.

ANITA: *(shamefully).* What did the Lord tell you about me, Daddy?

PASTOR: That you are sliding back into the world of lustful pleasures. That you have already compromised your faith in the Lord and are living in obstinacy and disobedience. So, I decided to come here and talk to you, and I met it as I was told. You didn't come to the church this evening.

ANITA: *(frowns)* I was in the church on Sunday.

PASTOR: Yes, and you sang in the Choir. I saw you. But this evening, you didn't show up.

ANITA: *(frowns with disinterest)* I was so choked up in the office today, so I couldn't come to the church.

PASTOR: Did you hear from your husband?

ANITA: *(with disinterest)* Yes, we spoke this evening. I told you he said he would go for the interview this morning at the Embassy. He did, but they didn't give him the visa again.

PASTOR: *(nods faintly)* That is why I am here.

ANITA: *(surprised)* How?

PASTOR: *(solemnly)* It is time to go back home.

ANITA: *(looks stern)* To where...?

PASTOR: It has been almost two years since you came into this city, and you have only lived with your husband just for two months before your big Uncle got you a visa to come here. You have hoped that your husband would join you, and the hope has gone on and on till now.

ANITA: I can't go back yet, Daddy; my papers are not yet complete.

PASTOR: Then leave the papers alone and go and build the home the Lord has given you. You've got to choose between completing the papers and building your home and living for God.

ANITA: *(displeased)* Did my husband call you to persuade me to abandon my work here and come home?

PASTOR: No, it wasn't your husband who spoke to me, it was God who sent me to go and warn you to desist from your ungodly life and do His will.

ANITA: I am not living an ungodly life, Daddy.

PASTOR: You are. He said your ways are not clean in His sight. You should fear an impending calamity

ANITA: Calamity? What calamity?

PASTOR: What do you think? Don't you think there will be a consequence for every act of ungodliness? (*looks displeased at the rebuke as she stands by the base of the staircase*) You left your husband back at home in the cold and began to live a wayward life here.

ANITA: *(grumbles)* That is not true, Daddy.

PASTOR: You attend parties and clubs and hang out with ungodly friends. Yet you serve at the Lord's altar. You belong to the Church Workers, and you sing in the choir. *(She looks at the man with surprise).* This evening, when I didn't see you in the church, the Spirit of God moved me to come to you and talk to you. *(He pauses)* Have you once heard of the Parable of the Ten Virgins?

ANITA: *(coldly)* Yes, Pastor. Five were wise and five were foolish.

PASTOR: *(bluntly)* Yes, and you belong to the foolish camp.

ANITA: Me?

PASTOR: Yes, your light has gone out and your lamp no longer has oil in it. You are empty inside of you and surrounded by darkness outside.

ANITA: *(stunned at the bluntness)* How?

PASTOR: The Lord impressed it on my heart to come and share a story with you so that you might understand how spiritually empty and physically gullible you are.

ANITA: A story...?

PASTOR: Yes, the story of an African prince, who called home urgently to come and attend to some of his father's business.

SCENE THREE

(Inside a large house, two men carry boxes down the staircase to a waiting car outside. Then, a fine-looking man in a suit, hat, and walking stick walks down the staircase into the large living room. He crosses the passage to the large living room where a young woman sits in tears. He moves closer to her, pulls her up to her feet, and holds her hands, while she looks away from him in protest.)

PRINCE: *(sweetly)* Come on, Victoria, look at me…just look at me. *(She turns her face to him)* It was because my father sent for me urgently, that I must go. He wants me to come and attend to some urgent business of his. I will be back soon.

VICTORIA: *(sadly)* Business, what business? Your father is a royal king, he has several subjects. He has aides and business associates, why didn't he call one of them to help manage his urgent business needs…Why you?

PRINCE: My Dear…because I was there when he began

the multi-national business. We started it together and I can fix the problems. *(Wiping her tears)*

VICTORIA: So, when are you coming back?

PRINCE: I will be back when the work is done. I believe it is going to be very soon.

VICTORIA: But how soon?

PRINCE: I will be back very soon, Honey. Please, hold on for me…Please…and take care of the children till I come back. *(He pulls her to himself and hugs her, while she remains sad)*

VICTORIA: Who will be with me while you are away?

PRINCE: Don't worry I will take care of that. I will send my twin brother to come and check on you. When I get home, I will send him to you. He will stay in this city with you and keep you company. *(Then, he begins to walk outside, as the woman escorts him to the large car. He enters the car, and as they wave to each other, the car zooms off. Painfully and reluctantly, the woman walks back into the house and locks the door.)*

SCENE FOUR

(Back in the house with Pastor and Anita. She still stands by the base of the staircase listening to the story.)

PASTOR: The Prince went on a long journey and left his wife behind, with a promise to be back very soon. Has that story begun to make any sense to you?

ANITA: *(shrugs indifferently)* Not really, yet.

PASTOR: Didn't Jesus say the same thing to all His disciples in John 14:1-3, when He said: "*Let not your heart be troubled: ye believe in God, believe also in me. In my father's house are many mansions: if it were not so, I would have told you. I am going to prepare a place for you. And if I go and prepare a place for you, I will come again, and receive you unto myself; that where I am, there ye may be also.*

ANITA: Yes, Daddy.

PASTOR: The prince never said exactly when he would return, but he assured his wife, he would come back

soonest. Is this story now making some sense?
ANITA: Yes.

PASTOR: Meanwhile, days rolled over days and months rolled into a year, and the wife of the prince still waited.

SCENE FIVE

(Sometime later, in the large house of the prince. His wife comes down the stairs into the kitchen. She looks dejected as she opens the fridge and brings out a bottle of water. Under deep reflection, she pours the water into the cup quietly and begins to sip the water, staring ahead of her in deep thought.)

VICTORIA: *(dejectedly)* I don't know when he is coming
(She goes to the window of the living room, parts the curtains sideways, and peeps outside. She leaves the window and begins to go back upstairs. Midway up the stairs, she hears someone knocking on the door. She rushes down and dashes to the door and opens it. She stands face to face with a young man dressed in a light cream suit. She feels a bit disappointed seeing someone else. The man smiles sweetly.)

THE MAN: *(smiling)* Hello...! I am Shalom.... Shalom Godwin. I disappointed you. I am not the person you expect to see.

VICTORIA: (*turning away from the door*) Yes, I was expecting my husband.

SHALOM: I know. He sent me to you.

VICTORIA: (*lightens up with excitement*) You know him? He sent you.

SHALOM: May I come inside?

VICTORIA: Oh, please, do. Come inside. (*She leads him to the living room and shows him a seat.*)

SHALOM: (*sitting down*) Thank you. I arrived yesterday from home. My brother sent his greetings.

VICTORIA: (*astonished*) Your brother...? Is he your brother?

SHALOM: (*smiling*) Twin brother; not identical though. Same father, same mother, same blood.

VICTORIA: How's my husband?

SHALOM: He sent his greetings. He is busy sorting out some problems in our father's company.

VICTORIA: (*sitting down and looking at him anxiously*) So when is he coming back? I miss him so much.

SHALOM: It is very difficult to say when he will come back. But his coming back is very sure. He told me, when he comes back, he will relocate his family back home.

VICTORIA: Relocation? We are all going back home with him.

SHALOM: That was what he said. We have a very big palace back home, and many servants too.

VICTORIA: *(pleased)* I will wait…! I can't wait to see him again. I miss him.

SHALOM: *(dipping his hand into his breast pocket, he brings out a folded paper)* He told me to give you this letter.

VICTORIA: *(screams with ecstasy)* Oh, my God! He wrote me a letter…! Oh! My God…!
She snatches the letter from him and hastily unfolds it and gazes at it with elation. She begins to read.)
My Dearest Victoria,

It has been six months since I left you and my children, and it has been like an eternity. I am sorry I had to leave you when I did; it was my father's business that demanded my attention. But you don't worry. I will make up for all my absence when I come back.

I sent my brother, Shalom, to inform you that I have decided to bring you all back here with me, so I won't have to leave you again. Here is a very large palatial residence for us. It is more comfortable here by all standards. I will come for you and the children very soon.

My brother, Shalom, will always come to visit you from time to time. And I will always send messages to you. I will be back soon. I miss you. I miss your companionship.

My heart is with you.
I love you dearly.
Your loving Husband,
Prince Emmanuel Godwin.

    (She finishes reading the letter and holds it to her chest in absolute joy. She sighs with relief.)

SHALOM: *(pleased)* So how do you feel now?

VICTORIA: I feel great. I feel on top of the world. I am pleased. I will wait for him.
    (Shalom dips his hand into his breast pocket and brings out a card. He gives it to her)

SHALOM: My brother commissioned me to see to your welfare and help you in all ways possible till he comes back. Here is my card. It contains my address and phone numbers. I have a house very close by, along the second street.

VICTORIA: That's very good. So, it will be easy for me to get in touch with you at any time.

SHALOM: I will be in touch with you from time to time.

SCENE SIX

(Back in Anita's house. She still stands by the base of the staircase, resting her back against the wooding rail in absolute concentration on the Pastor's story.)

PASTOR: He sent his twin brother to come and stay and watch over his wife. Does anything about "relocation" sounds familiar to you?

ANITA: "Relocation"?

PASTOR: The prince sent a message to his wife that he would come and relocate her to his palatial residence in his hometown.

ANITA: *(puzzled)* No, I don't know about any relocation.

PASTOR: Then, you are dull in understanding, Anita. Haven't you heard of these things many times in the church?

ANITA: I have never heard any teaching about "Relocation" in the church.

PASTOR: Yes, but you have heard about the Rapture of the Saints, about Jesus coming and taking His Bride away to be with Him forever. *(Anita stares at him confused)*

ANITA: *(trying to remember)* Yes, I think so.

PASTOR: *(speaks loudly to Anita)* "For the Lord Himself will descend from heaven with a shout, with the voice of an archangel, and with the trumpet of God. And the dead in Christ will rise first. Then we who are alive and remain shall be caught up together with them in the clouds to meet the Lord in the air. And thus, we shall always be with the Lord." I Thessalonians 4:16-17. That is like the "Relocation" the prince was talking about. In his palatial residence in his hometown.

SCENE SEVEN

(A YEAR LATER)
(Towards evening in Victoria's house, she sits on a couch watching a TV evangelist preach on the television. She sits despondently, looking discouraged and sad. Suddenly, there is a loud sound of the doorbell which jolts her into life. She turns in the direction of the door on her seat anxiously and speaks smilingly to herself:)

VICTORIA: At last,
(The doorbell sounds again, and she jumps to her feet, rushing towards the door) Hold on…I am coming! *(She gets to the door, unlocks it, and opens it; standing there and laughing heartily are two ladies in heavy facial make-up and weird attires and jewelry.)*

LADIES: *(laughingly)* Hello…!
 (She looks at them disappointedly with disinterest, and turns back from the door, coming back into the living room. The ladies, still smile as they enter the house and close the door behind them. They keep laughing as they follow her into the living room.)

HILARY: *(laughing loudly):* Come on, Baby, you are not cheerful at us? What is the matter?

SITANDA: *(jeeringly)* It is obvious we are not the person she was expecting. We disappointed her. Vicky, what's up?

VICTORIA: *(sharply)* Eh, Girls, what is the matter again? I have told you to leave me alone.

HILARY: Come on, Baby, we were together before; doing things in common, enjoying life together, painting the streets red with parties and lots and lots of boys and drinks…

SITANDA: Until your so-called Prince stole you away from us.

VICTORIA: He didn't steal me away; I chose to follow him and love him.

HILARY: Has he called you yet?

VICTORIA: *(coldly)* Yes, he wrote me a letter. *(They all burst into a loud derisive laughter. She looks at them with surprise)*

SITANDA: *(sneers with laughter)* He wrote her a letter when other husbands take their ladies out for picnics and cinemas and restaurants in highbrow parts of the city…Victoria's Prince wrote her a letter… *(they raise a loud jeering laughter again.)*

HILARY: Do you know what my man did to me on the last Valentine's Day? Vicky, my man took me to the Hilton Hotel and spoilt me with plates of sumptuous meals and pricey wine in splendid goblet inside a lavishly furnished suite in the hotel.

SITANDA: My affluent man-friend took me to the Caribbean Island, and there we were for two whole weeks!

HILARY: (*to Sitanda*) Whoa! Two weeks! You spent two weeks with Everest in the Caribbean? Whoa! You must have had a very long nice time together.

SITANDA: (*smiling*) Oh...yeah! We did! We had all the time to ourselves.

VICTORIA: My husband is coming back. He is coming to relocate us to live with Him in his palatial residence.

HILARY: When is he coming back? Did he tell you when?

VICTORIA: (*a bit puzzled*) No. He didn't. But he assured me, he would come back. (*The two friends erupt in a loud contemptuous laughter again*)

SITANDA: (*laughing scornfully*) Oh...my God...! Oh...my God....!

HILARY: (*moving to Victoria and shaking her shoulder*) Vicky, wake up! Wake up from your fairy tales...You have been wickedly deceived. The man is not coming back; neither is she coming to relocate you to any palatial residence. You are being seriously deceived. Wake up from your slumber and step out of this dungeon you called "a new life".

SITANDA: You are suffering here, Vicky. There are men out there who would be ready to die for you and give you all you want so that you might be their woman. Enough of all this stupid and thoughtless waiting.

HILARY: How are you sure the prince has not been going out with other ladies he could find around him…?

VICTORIA: *(harshly)* My husband is not like that, girls. He is a highly respectable personality. He would never lie to me.

SITANDA: *(pitifully)* I can't imagine why a very knowledgeable person as you are would simply believe that a Prince who had left you for more than a year now, would remain as he was without going out with other ladies there in his hometown. The man kept you standing while he went about dancing with other fine ladies. Wake up, Vicky.

HILARY: How is Lawrence?

VICTORIA: *(with indifference)* Which Lawrence?

HILARY: Come on, you know who I am talking about? Lawrence, your man…You had a lot of fun with him.

VICTORIA: *(rising with displeasure).* That was a thing of the past. It has no relevance to me anymore. Old things have passed away, girls.

HILARY: Just to let you know that the man has hooked up with another lady now.

VICTORIA: Which man?

SITANDA: (*laughs*) Lawrence, of course. You dropped him; another lady picked him up. One man's poison is another man's meat. They just came back from The Bahamas.

VICTORIA: (*enviously*) To do what?

SITANDA: On a 10-day cruise, of course.

HILARY: You see what I mean? It is sheer silliness, giving your love to a man who has no time for you. Wake up, Vicky. Come out of this dungeon you call "new life" into a world of great freedom and pleasure.   (*Victoria walks to the window contemplatively and stands gazing outside.*)

VICTORIA: (*pensively*) Girls, I need to be alone. I need some time to think. (*The entrance door opens, and Shalom walks inside. He looks displeased seeing the visitors. Victoria turns to the girls sternly*) Girls, you need to leave now?

HILARY: (*surprised*) Won't you introduce this man to us?

VICTORIA: He is Shalom, my husband's twin brother.

He lives close by and has been here to help me and keep me company till my husband comes.

SITANDA: (*sneers*) He was sent to hinder you from enjoying your life while the prince abandoned you here and is enjoying himself with the ladies of hometown.?

VICTORIA: (*calmly with a strong voice*) Girls, please, leave now.

HILARY: Can we come for you this evening? There is a real party in town, and we shall all be there.

VICTORIA: Just leave now. (*The friends carry their handbags and walk past Shalom who still stands sternly watching them. They go out of the house, looking displeased at Victoria who still stands by the window. After they have gone out of the house, Shalom turns in the direction of Victoria*)

SHALOM: (*solemnly*) Victoria, who are those ladies?

VICTORIA: (*still looking away from Shalom with disrespect*) My friends. Do you have any problem with them?

SHALOM: (*with concern*) Those are not the type of friends you are to keep if you want to…

VICTORIA: (*cutting in angrily*) Shalom, when will your brother come back to me?

SHALOM: (*deep-heartedly*) Victoria, your husband is

coming back soon. He spoke to me again this afternoon and told me to assure you again of his coming, but you will need to patiently hold on. He said he was trying to explain to you in the afternoon, but you were impatient with him.

VICTORIA: (*harshly*) I am tired of this waiting–game. I can't keep on waiting for a man who has no definite time to come back. I hate this endless wait. Things are happening outside of this cocoon. A lot of life is passing me by. I am missing things and yet all I get is a promise of a "relocation" to a beautiful home sometimes when he comes back. I am fed up with all these empty promises and endless waits. (*Shalom comes to a seat closer to her*)

SHALOM: All these are not empty promises, Victoria. I came from there and it is real. But if you allow those types of ungodly friends with worldly lusts and desires, they will make you lose interest in the glorious things prepared for you by your husband.

VICTORIA: For how long do I have to wait? My patience is running out.

SHALOM: No, Victoria. You've got to hold on.

VICTORIA: (*sharply*) Till when? When is he coming back?

SHALOM: (*calmly*) He is coming back soon?

VICTORIA: (*shouts hotly*) I am tired of this endless wait! (*She hisses disgustedly, leaves Shalom's presence, and*

dashes into the adjacent room in anger. Shalom stands
speechlessly, looking.)

SCENE EIGHT

(Back in Anita's house. She is sitting in a seat opposite the elderly Pastor. She looks so sober by now, looking away from him guiltily)

PASTOR: Wrong association. Listening to ungodly counsels; standing in the ways of sinners and sitting in the seats of the scorners. Is it not interesting to know that your life is almost like what was happening to that woman?

ANITA: *(barefacedly)* No, Daddy.

PASTOR: No? You gradually began to open the door of your hearts to your unbelieving friends who kept on enticing you to step out of the covering of your Lord and Master into the sinful freedom of the world. They began to influence you to abandon your faith. You began to combine church attendance with a series of night parties; you began to mix your love for Jesus with love for sinful pleasure. You began to listen to your worldly friends who were reducing your love for your Lord and Master. So, the wife of the prince began to become seriously impatient.

SCENE NINE

AFTER THREE YEARS

(It is afternoon in Victoria's house. And a tall handsome young man, in highly fashionable loose top and well-tailored pants stands near the cabinet. A briefcase lies on the center table before him. Victoria stands near the window, looking displeased during a conversation.)

VICTORIA: *(shaking her head in disagreement)* Nelson, …Sorry, I want to remain loyal to my husband, I can't go out with you.

NELSON: *(shakes his head pitifully)* Vicky, you are waiting for a man who has abandoned you for almost six years now? You still hold on to the love for a man who has been enjoying himself back at home with other ladies he finds around? *(He bends down, and flings open the cover of the briefcase. It contains bundles of 100-dollar bills.)* I am offering my deep love and money to lavish on you. What else do you want me to do to show that I do love you? *(Victoria looks at the man and the briefcase full of money. She comes back to a seat and sits quietly in deep thought.)*

VICTORIA: *(solemnly)* What do you want from me, Nelson?

NELSON: My love, let me take you out. Let me show you how much I love you. (*Nelson, moves closer to her and holds her hand lovingly*) Victoria, come with me.

VICTORIA: *(contemplatively)* Nelson.

NELSON: *(still holding her hand)* Yes, my love.

VICTORIA: Can you give me time to think over this?

NELSON: *(in low spirit)* Sure, my love. I will give you time. But whenever you want to think about me, think of a man who loves you and will not abandon you. Think of a man who will lavish you with love, care, and money. We shall spend our honeymoon on a 7-day long cruise. We shall spend our vacations in plush hotels in Italy or Singapore or any cities of your choice in the Caribbean Islands. Think of a man dying to love you.

VICTORIA: *(smiles faintly, as they still hold hands)* Just give me a little time, Nelson, please.

NELSON: *(smiles sweetly)* But may I ....?

VICTORIA: *(smilingly looks at him)* Do what....?

NELSON: *(playfully)* Hug you or give you...just a peck?

VICTORIA: *(laughs and takes her hands away from him)*

No, come on, I have not made up my mind yet. Just give me the time to think it over.

NELSON: *(jovially)* I know what I will do to you.

VICTORIA: *(laughs)* What? Will you drag me to the altar in the dream?

NELSON: I will appear to you in dreams and chase you about and carry you in my arms and we shall cruise together over the whole city on Arabian flying carpet and....

VICTORIA: *(shouts with laughter)* No, stop flattering me, Nelson...Cruising over the city on an Arabian flying carpet...?

NELSON: *(begins to go to the door)* I will be back tomorrow evening to take my reply. Is that alright with you?

VICTORIA: *(sees the briefcase)* You forgot something.... the briefcase.

NELSON: I brought it for you. I can't go back with it. It's yours, Victoria.

VICTORIA: *(astounded)* You leave it for me...? All this money! But I have not said either yes or no.

NELSON: Even if you later decide to say know...it is a gift from my heart...a testimony to my deep love. *(He gets to the door, opens it, and steps out, while*

Victoria stands looking at the box of 100-dollar bills. Suddenly, Shalom walks inside from a corner of the house. Victoria is shocked.)

VICTORIA: Shalom, when did you walk into the house? *(a bit hotly)* You have been eavesdropping on me?

SHALOM: I came inside when you were talking, I thought you saw me. I was sitting in the kitchen because I didn't want to disturb your conversation. *(Victoria goes to the briefcase and closes it. She carries it and begins to go towards the stairs.)* Victoria, which briefcase is that, and who was that man? Do you know him?

VICTORIA: *(harshly)* I don't think I am under obligation to let you know about each visitor or guest I receive in this house. And it is none of your business, whoever I befriend or gives me a gift. *(She moves to the stairs and Shalom stops her again.)*

SHALOM: That man has come to deceive you into abandoning your husband, the prince, and marrying him, isn't it? I beg you. That man is a deceiver. He is your enemy, the enemy of your glorious destiny. Don't do it.

VICTORIA: *(angrily)* Don't do what?

SHALOM: Your husband will come very soon. He will come and take you to his large palatial mansion in his hometown. He has…

VICTORIA: *(shouts madly)* Stop fooling me with an empty and hopeless promise. Stop deceiving me to wait for a man who has no more interest in me. Is he really coming back? I don't believe so.

SHALOM: But he has assured you that....

VICTORIA: No-o-o-o! (*She begins to climb the stairs with the briefcase in her hand. Shalom looks at her speechlessly*)

SCENE TEN

(Anita, with her head bowed in soberness, still listens to the Pastor's story.)

PASTOR: The wife of the prince took the gift from the man. It is a gradual compromise. That is like your case. Influence of worldly friends and love for lustful desires began to overwhelm you till you gradually started to slide into lustful pleasures. You remain in the church, yes, but there are no clear demarcations between you and your unbeliever friends. You attend parties with them, where you too have fun dancing with the husbands of other women. Gradually, you began to lose interest in the things of God. And then, you began to sleep with other men without any trace of guilt in you. You began to abandon your faith in the Lord? The sins you hated before suddenly started to appeal to your taste.

SCENE ELEVEN

(It is the middle of the night in Victoria's house. She lies on her bed in her bedroom, holding a pillow to her bosom with her tearful eyes opened in the room dimly lit with the ray of light filtering inside through the silky window curtains. Tears stream down her face as she stares blankly at the empty ceiling of her room. Once a while, she turns about on the bed; then, she begins to think aloud)

VICTORIA: It has been long since he left me behind. He sent his twin brother to watch over me and be with me, but what is that to being with him and having him around? Am I not wasting away? Am I not missing a lot? I have rejected the loving hands of many handsome men who are dying to date me. All in the name of waiting for a prince who has no date of returning. *(The sharp ringing of her phone startles her. She quickly picks up the phone on the bedside stool.)*

Yes, who is this?

(It is the prince, sitting inside a large garden. Two young men in formal uniform attire stand around in the garden as his attendants. He is on the phone.)

PRINCE: Hello…Honey…

VICTORIA: (*dispiritingly*) Yes, dear.

PRINCE: What is happening…? You no longer sound jubilant as you used to do…You have lost your inspiration and joy…You no longer listen to me with excitement as you used to do before. I do hope you are not getting discouraged about my long delay.

VICTORIA: (*sharply*) I am…I am becoming uncomfortable with your long delay.

PRINCE: No, my darling wife, do not be discouraged. Hold on for me, I am almost rounding off my assignment here.

VICTORIA: (*sternly with some indifference*) My dear husband, You have not been able to satisfy my question. You must be definite.

PRINCE: On what?

VICTORIA: Tell me, when exactly are you coming back to be with me?

PRINCE: I am not only coming back to you, but I am coming back to take you with me back home here. The palatial residence is here, and the servants to do your bidding are here. It is a very large kingdom here and my father is the king, while I am the heir to the throne. (*He smiles proudly*) And you shall be a royal Queen sitting beside me all the time.

VICTORIA: *(angrily)* I have heard enough of those promises. You have bored me with those empty promises that have no definite time of fulfillment. I am fed up with them, and they make no meaning to me again.

PRINCE: But I am surely coming back to you.

VICTORIA: When?

PRINCE: My father has not told me. But by all indications, I could be ordered to come any moment from now.

VICTORIA: *(disrespectfully)* I am getting wearied by the day, Prince. I don't know what to do again.

PRINCE: No, you must wait.... Hello...! Hello...! *(Victoria still holds the receiver to her ear, but remains quiet, without saying anything as the prince calls at the other end)* Hello...Victoria...Victoria....

SCENE TWELVE

(It is towards evening in Victoria's house. She stands by the window, gazing outside anxiously and glancing at the wall clock at intervals.)

VICTORIA: *(talking to herself impatiently)* Am I crazy? Am I not running mad for waiting endlessly for a man who has broken his promises of coming back? Will I continue to wait like this in this slavery I called freedom? *(The sharp sound of the doorbell rattles her. She pauses in fright and high expectation. The doorbell sounds again. She begins to whisper to herself.)* Is that him? Is that my Prince? Is he? *(She sneaks to the door and quietly opens the door to the person. Nelson walks inside again. Victoria stands looking at him speechlessly)*

NELSON: *(with a faint smile)* I am back, Victoria.

VICTORIA: I wasn't expecting you, Nelson.

NELSON: *(goes to a seat)* And who are you expecting? A man who has abandoned you for the past five or six years. A man who covers up his infidelity by just flattering you over the phone. I have presented myself to you and made you a promise and I am making a covenant with you that I will not abandon you. I will love you so dearly and care for you with everything I have. I have come to receive an answer to my request. *(Victoria becomes confused again. She goes to the window again and looks out.)* Victoria, please, look at me.... Look at me. *(She turns to Nelson with tearful eyes.)* Victoria, do something for me.

VICTORIA: *(somberly)* What?

NELSON: Tell me you don't love me; and I will leave your house now, never to return. Tell me you have no love for me, and I will trouble you no more. *(There is a long silence between them. Then, Nelson stands up quietly and begins to go to the main entrance. Victoria stands looking indecisively till he gets to the door. As he puts his hands on the knob to open the door, Victoria speaks out, tears well up in her eyes.)*

VICTORIA: Wait, Nelson. *(Nelson pauses at the door and turns back to her. Then she stammers out her words)* Don't go.   I...am confused.

NELSON: So am I, Victoria. I am more confused than you. I don't know what else to do to show you how deep my love for you is. I have done all I could do to express my love for you, but you doubted me because a useless man who has never fulfilled a promise has disappointed you. I am confused. *(He *opens the door to go out. Victoria quickly calls him)*

VICTORIA: Wait...!   *(Nelson pauses again, the door already opened. And she speaks with a trembling voice.)* I.... will.

NELSON: *(lightens up. He gently closes back the door.)* Come out more clearly, Victoria. *(Still with tears in her eyes, she walks past Nelson and begins to go upstairs, halfway up, she pauses again and turns to Nelson)*

VICTORIA: Wait for me.

NELSON: *(smiles with a bow)* Yes, my love. *(He comes back to sit in a chair. Victoria goes up the stairs. She enters her bedroom, looks straight before her in a deep thought, then, quietly, and musingly removes the ring on her finger and throws it aside.*
Shortly later, she came down the stairs, looking glamorous in flashy attire, heavy make-up, and pieces of jewelry. Nelson sees her and rises from his seat in admiration. She comes into the living room while Nelson gazes at her dazzling beauty in utter amazement.)*

VICTORIA: I am set.

NELSON: *(still looking astonished)* For what, my love?

VICTORIA: Take me out for dinner. I want to go out with you.

NELSON: *(smiles sweetly as he bows lovingly to her)* This is all I have prayed for. This is my dream coming to pass before my very eyes.

VICTORIA: *(happily, turning round to show him herself)* How do I look?

NELSON: *(he holds her hands admiringly)* Trendy…! You look glamorous in a dazzling beauty! You look gorgeous in your exquisite attire! You are more beautiful than I have ever seen you in my life! *(Goes walking round her, admiring her, while she stands smiling shyly)* Come on, have I ever seen a lady as stunning as this…? Have I ever seen….?

VICTORIA: *(cuts in with a laugh)* Enough of all the flatters…!

NELSON: Where do you want me to take you for the dinner?

VICTORIA: Anywhere.

NELSON: I will take you to the dining room of the best 5-star hotel in the city where I will spoil you with the most flavorsome delicacies. Then we shall have all the time for ourselves. *(Holds her hand)* Shall we move?

VICTORIA: Yes, Nelson. I have waited for all these for a long time. *(They walk towards the door. Then, the door opens from outside and Shalom walks in and remains shocked as he stands by the door.)*

SHALOM: Victoria...!

VICTORIA: *(disrespectfully)* I never expected to see you at this time.

SHALOM: *(in shock)* What is going on?

VICTORIA: I am moving on. Your brother is not coming back again. I can't wait any longer for a man who has no respect for promises.

SHALOM: My brother, your Prince, has respect for promises. He never broke vows, and he will keep all the promises he has ever made with you. But you must be patient.

VICTORIA: *(hotly)* Till when?

SHALOM: *(persuasively)* He is coming back very soon.

VICTORIA: *(obstinately)* I do not believe that theory anymore. Enough of this waiting game.

SHALOM: *(points to Nelson)* This man, I know him very well. He is an enemy of your destiny. Don't go with him. This man is...

NELSON: *(to Victoria)* He is only covering up for his deceitful, disloyal, and treacherous brother. Both are timewasters.

VICTORIA: *(to Shalom)* You and your brother are time wasters. *(Touching Nelson)* He is the best thing that has ever happened to me.

SHALOM: Don't allow this deceiver into your life. He is your enemy and the enemy of your husband. Your husband is coming back very soon. From all indications, he could arrive at any time. There are signals everywhere around to show that he will come very soon.

VICTORIA: Those signals have been everywhere around ever since.

(Turning to Nelson) Shall we go? *(Nelson holds her hand and together, they walk out of the living room to the driveway outside where Nelson has parked his big expensive car. Shalom comes out of the house, looking at them in utter bewilderment, as Nelson helps Victoria to the front seat and he goes to the driver's seat, starts the engine, and drives off.)*

SCENE THIRTEEN

(In Anita's house. She still stands resting her back against the wooden rail of the staircase. She wipes her wet eyes with the sleeve of her blouse. The elderly Pastor still talks to her bluntly)

PASTOR: Do you know what Apostle Peter prophesied to us in his epistles 2 Peter 3:3-4?

"Knowing this first: that scoffers will come in the last days, walking according to their lusts, and saying, "Where is the promise of His coming? For since the fathers fell asleep, all things continue as they were from the beginning of creation."

But he spoke further in verses 9-10:

"The Lord is not slack concerning His promise, as some count slackness, but is longsuffering toward us, not willing that any should perish but that all should come to repentance. But the day of the Lord will come as a thief in the night, in which the heavens will pass away with a great noise, and the elements will melt with fervent heat; both the earth and the works that are in it will be burned up."

Many believers like you have ignored the warnings

of the Holy Spirit and have dumped their spiritual commitment in the garbage bin. You and others like you no longer believe that the Lord Jesus Christ would come as he has promised. So, like the five Foolish Virgins, their oil has dried up and they are empty inside. You and others like you have suddenly forgotten about heaven and have refused to keep themselves holy for the coming of their Lord and Master.

SCENE FOURTEEN

(Nelson's car pulls up in the parking lot of a large hotel. He steps down from the car and hurries to the door of the front seat; he opens the door for Victoria and playfully bows reverently for her. She laughs timidly and slaps his hand. He closes the door, and hand in hand, they walk into the lobby of the large hotel.
Shortly later, they are sitting opposite each other, with plates of food and glass cups of wine in between them. A small red love- candle burns in a glassy candle stand. They eat and talk, laughing. Soft music plays on in the background. Other people walk about around them. Then, Nelson dips his hand in his breast pocket and brings out a tiny box tied in red ribbon.)

NELSON: *(smile)* I brought for you the greatest gift I have ever given a person.

VICTORIA: *(getting excited)* What is that? *(Nelson gives it to her, and she collects it with trembling hands. With her mounting excitement, she asks him)* My God…What is this, Nelson?

NELSON: *(teasingly)* It is a surprise. Open the box and see, my love. *(Victoria quietly untied the ribbon and opened the tiny box. His face lightens up in astonishment.)*

VICTORIA: *(gives a short scream)* Oh…! My God…! Oh…my God.! *(It is a golden engagement ring. She is dumbfounded as Nelson takes the box from her hand, quietly removes the ring from the hold and gently holds her finger and inserts the ring, and kisses it lightly.*

NELSON: *(solemnly)* Will you… marry me? I will take care of you. I will cherish you and will not abandon you, till death do us part. Please…don't tell me: No. *(Pause as Victoria stares at Nelson with a smile and glances at the ring with admiration. Then, she springs up from her seat, comes to Nelson, and hugs him)*

VICTORIA: Yes, I do.

NELSON: *(Yells excitedly)* Yeah…! Yeah…! I love you, my love.

VICTORIA: I love you too.

NELSON: You know what?

VICTORIA: *(still looking at the ring)* You tell me.

NELSON: I have booked a Royal Suite.

VICTORIA: I thought we were going to your house.

NELSON: Today is a special day, my love. And this evening is the most special evening I have waited for all my life. Proposing to an angel of my dream…a lady of unequaled beauty. Let's stay here this evening and spend time together without distractions, Honey.

VICTORIA: *(nods with a smile)* OK, agreed.

NELSON: We need to order for a bottle of champagne. We need to celebrate, my love. *(He beckons to a waiter.)*

SCENE FIFTEEN

(The next morning, in the hotel suite. Victoria is lying on the bed, the bed cover covering her up below her neck. Nelson comes out of the bathroom already dressed up. He goes to Victoria, and taps her feet to wake her up)

NELSON: Vicky, …wake up. Wake up…it's time to go.
(She stirs and opens her eyes, sees Nelson already dressed up and looks to be in a hurry)

VICTORIA: Nelson, where are you going? You are already dressed.

NELSON: *(wearing his socks)* I just remembered I must keep an appointment with a business associate.

VICTORIA: *(looks puzzled)* An appointment? You just remembered?

NELSON: Yes, my dear. I've got to keep it.

VICTORIA: *(still looking dazed)* So? What happened? I have to wait for you here.

NELSON: *(bluntly)* No. We are checking out right away.

VICTORIA: *(becoming more confused)* But you told me last night that you have got this suite for three days. You said we shall have fun together and enjoy ourselves together for three days.... You said we have all the days to ourselves. How come you are cutting short this pleasurable moment?

NELSON: *(smiles faintly as he buttons his sleeves)* The honeymoon is simply over, Sweetie. It's time to go home. (*She looks dumbfounded at his sudden change of attitude. She sits up on the bed, looking at him with astonishment.*)

VICTORIA: *(almost inaudibly)* Taking me to your house?

NELSON: No. That will be later. I will come and see you in your house later today.

VICTORIA: Nelson, you are behaving strangely. You are completely different from yesterday. What has happened?

NELSON: I will discuss it with you later. But we have to leave now.   (*With a more confused mind, she still gazes at Nelson.*) Sweetie, I am sorry I must catch up with this appointment. Please, drop the keycard at the Front Office when you leave the room. (*He carries his briefcase and a bag and goes to the door. Victoria watches him dreamily, as he opens the door.*)

VICTORIA: *(voices out with almost in tears)* Nelson. You are leaving me?

NELSON: I told you I have an urgent appointment to keep. *(He opens the door and steps out and closes the door behind him. Victoria still stares astounded, at the closed door.)*

SCENE SIXTEEN

(Victoria arrives in a taxicab in front of her house and becomes surprised to see a strange large white car in the driveway of her house. Standing beside the car are two young men in light-cream suit and uniform shirts and ties. They stand firm, without moving or exchanging greetings with her as she approaches the entrance of the house with fear and caution. She opens the door and steps inside. She walks into the living room and freezes in shock as she sees the prince, in a light cream gorgeous suit sitting down on the seat with his golden walking stick; Shalom sits quietly beside him. They both watch Victoria walking inside speechlessly. She stands before them completely astounded, visibly shivering; then, she stirs up and moves towards the prince to hug him.)

VICTORIA: Eh! My Prince…! My Prince…!

PRINCE: *(holds up his hand with a stern face.)* Eh…! Stop! *(Victoria pauses midway instantly. Silence, as the prince scans her with his eyes.)* Princess Victoria, you betrayed me!

VICTORIA: *(stammers in fear)* No, my Prince…No…I didn't …

PRINCE: *(solemnly)* Yes, my princess, you did. You have been deceived by my enemy not to wait for me.

VICTORIA: No, my Prince…no, my Prince…

PRINCE: I can smell unrighteousness all over you. As you were approaching me, I could smell your unfaithfulness to our marriage vows. Who have you been with?

VICTORIA: *(trembling)* I just went out with a friend, my Prince.

PRINCE: *(shakes his head pitifully)* Unfortunately not. He is not a friend. He is not who you think he is. You have been with Nelson. *(Victoria expresses shock).*

VICTORIA: *(faintheartedly)* You know him…? My Prince knows him…?

PRINCE: *(shakes his head disappointedly).* You have been fooled.

VICTORIA: *(alarmed)* Oh…My Prince…!

PRINCE: Nelson was my father's chief servant back at home!

VICTORIA: What…!

PRINCE: He had served in the palace for many years. Then he suddenly began to corrupt many of my father's servants and workers, instigating them against my father's authority. He spread rebellion and obstinacy against the throne of my father. Then he was sacked.

VICTORIA: *(bursts into tears. She speaks breathlessly)* Oh...! I can't believe this...!

PRINCE: *(sternly)* Even while I still tell you the truth.? You still can't believe? No wonder you didn't believe I would come back as I promised. When he was sacked, he stole a lot of money from inside the Palace. I knew he had given you some money to deceive you. He stole whatever he gave you; they all belonged to my father. (*He sees the ring on her finger.*) What is that on your finger? Engagement ring? He gave you that. And where is the one I gave you? So, you are now engaged to him, and you have defiled yourself with him.

VICTORIA: *(crying bitterly)* I..am sorry...my Prince...

PRINCE: You know what? Nelson came into this city on a revenge mission. He knew you were my delight. He knew I was building a new palatial mansion, a wonderful castle for you and me. He knew I was making a lot of preparations back at home to come here and relocate you back to my place. He knew all these, but he wanted to avenge his termination of employment; he wanted to even the score with me...he wanted to strike me where it would hit me most, so he decided to come and deceive you and defile you before I came. And he got you.

VICTORIA: *(sobbing bitterly)* I didn't ...know. I am...sorry, my Prince...

PRINCE: But I knew Shalom warned you. He told you the man is your enemy, who came to deceive you out of your glorious future.
(One of the servants standing outside walks in and speaks reverently with a bow)

SERVANT: They are here, sir. They got him.

PRINCE: That is very good. *(He stands up quietly and walks towards the door. He turns to Victoria)* Come out here and see the futility of your foolish wisdom. *(Victoria follows the prince out of the house, and they come outside, she sees Nelson standing in between two police officers. He is handcuffed. Victoria screams in shock when she sees him.)*

POLICEMAN I: We just brought him to confirm to you that we got him. He was trying to cross the border and escape, but we got him. We are charging him to court, and he is heading straight to jail.

PRINCE: Good job, officers. That's a good job. Thanks very much.
(The policemen push him back into the car. They enter the car and drive off. Victoria continues in bitter tears. The prince walks gently towards his car and Shalom follows him.)

VICTORIA: *(crying aloud)* My Prince...! Oh...! My Prince...don't go. Don't leave me. Take me with you to your Palace...! Oh...I am sorry! *(She wants to rush forward to the prince, but the stern-looking servants block her way and push her back. The servants open the door of the car for the prince. He enters the car without looking at Victoria. Shalom sits beside him. They start the car, and the car begins to go, as Victoria begins to wail loudly.)* Oh...! I miss my glorious destiny! Ah! I was deceived...! Ah...I am finished...! I miss it...!

SCENE SEVENTEEN

(Anita is now sobbing profusely. She stands by the wooden rail of the staircase and sobs at the rebuke and the story of the elderly Pastor.)

PASTOR: In Mark 13:35, Jesus Christ says:
"Watch therefore, for you do not know when the master of the house is coming--in the evening, at midnight, at the crowing of the rooster, or in the morning"
All those who are not expecting his coming will cry bitterly when the trumpet sounds for the Rapture of His saints. There are people like you in the church of God who are among the Foolish Virgins. They cover their sinful life with a cloak of service. They serve in the church without heaven in view. They sing in the choir, teach in the church, pastor a congregation, and lead a ministry, but yet possess a heart engrossed in sins. This is what the Lord said to us in His word in Revelation 22:11-12,
"He who is unjust, let him be unjust still; he who is filthy, let him be filthy still; he who is righteous, let him be righteous still; he who is holy, let him be holy

still. And behold, I am coming quickly, and My reward is with Me, to give to every one according to his work."

I think this is what the Lord said I should come and tell you. To forsake your backslidden ways of life and retrace your steps back to him. (The Pastor rises quietly to go, Anita remains standing by the rail, still sobbing. Pastor goes to the door, opens it, and steps out of the house into the cold night outside. Anita begins to go upstairs sobbing. She enters her bedroom and falls on the bed in tears.)

SCENE EIGHTEEN

(It is around the sunset in Anita's House. She comes into the house, carrying her handbag. She seems to be arriving from work. She throws her handbag on the couch and goes to the kitchen area. Eunice, her friend is making some food on the cooker.)

EUNICE: Tired? Welcome.

ANITA: You came back from work so early. I never expected that.

EUNICE: I came home in time for the Church Workers' meeting. Daddy said he wanted to talk with us. Have you forgotten?

ANITA: *(frowns with disinterest)* Well, I may not be able to go to the meeting. I have an appointment in about an hour.

EUNICE: But Daddy will ask of you.

ANITA: Tell him I have been busy in the office, or just

say something to cover up for me.

EUNICE: You should know I can't tell a lie, worst still, to a man of God, my Pastor.

ANITA: *(shrugs indifferently)* Well, I have an appointment. I can't make the meeting this evening.

EUNICE: A man came in a few minutes before you came. He said he was Larry.

ANITA: Oh…God! Larry! That's him! What did he say?

EUNICE: He just came in and asked of you. He said you should meet him at the place.

ANITA: Which place?

EUNICE: He said: the Place. You should know the place, don't you? *(Anita turns back to go upstairs)* Anita. *(She pauses at the base of the stairs.)* Why are you living a double life?

ANITA: Double life? I don't know what you mean, Eunice.

EUNICE: *(with concern)* You profess to know the Lord Jesus Christ, yet you deny Him by the works of your hand.

ANITA: *(defensively)* Are you judging me?

EUNICE: No, Anita. I am not. I am only feeling concerned for you. I am just sad about …. *(Suddenly, there is a heavy sound, and she disappears from Anita's sight, and the dishes she is holding crash on the floor with all the clothes she wears. Anita staggers back with a scream. Then there is a dead silence everywhere for about two minutes, and then, shouts and screams begin to come from places around. Anita looks dumbfounded for a moment, completely terrified.)*

ANITA: *(screams aloud)* Oh…No-o-o-o! Eunice…! What happened? No-o-o-o! *(She rushes out of the kitchen into the living room; dashes up the stairs madly and rushes down again, shouting)* What… is… happening…? My God…! Eh…! Eh-e-e-e! *(She runs to the door, opens it, and looks outside, she sees a neighbor running into his car and speeding away. She runs to the side of the road and looks around. Some noises and screams come from nearby and distant houses in the neighborhood. She runs back into the house and puts on the TV to a news channel. She watches in horror as the newscaster talks about the sudden disappearance of some people a short moment ago.)* No-o-o-o-o! I am finished!
(She springs up from her bed where she had fallen after the Pastor had finished talking with her. The Rapture event has been a dream. She wakes up sweating and panting heavily) It's a dream! Thank God, it's a dream! Jesus have mercy on me-e-e-e-e!
(She drops to her knees panting with fear and trembling and raises her hands tearfully in absolute submission.)

THE END

"And behold, I am coming quickly, and My reward is with Me, to give to everyone according to his work.
"I am the Alpha and the Omega, the Beginning and the End, the First and the Last."
Blessed are those who do His commandments, that they may have the right to the Tree of Life and may enter through the gates into the city.
But outside are dogs and sorcerers and sexually immoral and murderers and idolaters, and whoever loves and practices a lie."

Just because He has delayed His coming so greatly does not mean that his coming will still be delayed. He is coming so soon. Sooner now than all the past warnings. Sins are getting more enticing, and the way of Holiness is getting more unpopular, yet, He had declared that no unclean person will enter his Kingdom. This drama piece is written to encourage all true believers not to stop living for God; it is to sound an alarm of the imminent of His coming. This dramatic piece is written to warn all children of God to resist the subtle temptations of the devil and to be steadfast against compromising their faith in their daily lives.

"Waiting for The Prince" is written by the inspiration of the Holy Spirit to encourage every believer in the Lord Jesus Christ not to be weary of expecting the coming of the Lord. They are to live their daily life with Heaven in view. For His coming, the Rapture, the sound of the Trumpet, will be so sudden and it is very close.

Prayerfully proceed to the next dramatic presentation: *"Tribulation Night"*.

Tribulation Night

By:

____

MIKE BAMILOYE

CHARACTERS

REV. NICHOLAS
DAVIES
AUGUSTINA
BETTY
MAURICE
NICHOLAS' WIFE
THREE CHILDREN of Nicholas
SIS DEBBY (Wife of Deacon Edward)
VERONICA (Daughter of Deacon Edward)
MERCY
HELENA (Nicholas' Secretary)
REV. HERBERT
GRANDMA
UNCLE SEYE
THE PASTORS (with Pastor Herbert)
A WOMAN (Scene 15)
SECURITY OFFICER 1
SUNDAY (Gateman)
OFFICER 1
OFFICER 2
OFFICER 3
2 SECURITY OPERATIVES
2 TORTURING OFFICERS
2 DEAD BODIES
4-ARMED MEN AT TORTURE SCENE

Prologue

(Davies and Maurice are running along a dusty road, then they look back and see the Police coming behind them. They branch into a nearby bush as the armed men pursue them and shoot. Maurice is hit. He screams, staggers, and begins to limp on the run. Davies runs back to him and begins to pull him along)

MAURICE: Davies, I've been hit.

DAVIES: I know, try more. Let's get out of their sight.
   (As they continue to drag along, another shot hits Maurice at the back, and he falls. Davies bends to carry him.)

MAURICE: *(faintly)* Davies…Go! Go! Leave me alone. *(Then he grabs his shirt and speaks quickly but faintly)* Davies, don't forget all that I have told you…whatever happens, it is better to die than take the Mark. Don't take the Mark… (In tears, Davies leaves him and runs away from the scene. Maurice pulls up himself and rests his back by a tree as the three-armed men arrive.)*

OFFICER 1: You are under arrest.

MAURICE: *(dying, smiles faintly)* It's too late. Thanks for the shot, guys. *(Then, he holds his side in agony)* Ah...thank you, Jesus...Thank you, Jesus... *(He dies. The Police shake his motionless body)*

OFFICER 1: Come on, let's go... Go! Get the other man. *(They leave him and pursue the other man.)*

SCENE ONE

(In the dead night, Davies is running through a footpath towards a large old, uncompleted building in a remote place away from the city. He holds the black nylon bag as he runs along towards the large house under the shining moonlight of the night. He gets there and steps inside cautiously, looking around heedfully. Then he goes to settle in a corner, sitting down wearily. He opens the bag brings out a half loaf of bread and begins to eat as he rests his back on the wall, exhausted.
From another part of the building, a man had heard footsteps and had been afraid. He looks so scared as he glues himself into the shadow of a corner of the dirty room he hides. Then, he sneaks out of the dark and tiptoes to a window overlooking the room the first man had sat down. The first man who had been sitting tiredly sees a shadowy figure and rushes up to run away, the second man calls)

2ND MAN:: *(whispers aloud)* Eh! Stop! I am hiding too! *(The first man freezes his movement)* Don't run away. Are you a believer?

1ST MAN: *(not turning his face yet)* And who are you?

2ND MAN: I am a believer. I have been hiding here for three days.

1ST MAN: *(solemnly)* I missed the great event too. My parents and my siblings are all gone. *(Then he turns round to face the man in the shadow. They pause and stare at each other for a moment, the first man expresses shock as he recognizes him)*

2ND MAN:: *(sadly)* What is it?

1ST MAN: *(still in shock)* Oh…my God! Oh…my God! I know this face… *(the second man turns back shamefully to leave. He calls him again)* Rev. (Dr.) Nicholas! I know you on the television…Please, don't go. *(Nicholas pauses, still looking away. The other man still talks with absolute astonishment)* Your many messages, your several teachings, and numerous Christian leadership conferences and Ministers' Seminars…. What happened?
  (Nicholas slowly turns to the man, his eyes wet with tears.)

NICHOLAS: *(sorrowfully)* The Rapture came and went, and the wheat and the tares were separated. The true believers left, and all the fake Christians and ministers showed their true faces.

1ST MAN: *(amazed)* I can't believe this.

NICHOLAS: What is it you cannot believe, my brother? Is

it the Word of Jesus in Matthew 7: 21 which says: *"Not everyone who says to Me, 'Lord, Lord,' shall enter the kingdom of heaven, but he who does the will of My Father in heaven?"* Or the confirmation of this word by John in the Book of Revelation 21:27 which says: *"But there shall by no means enter it anything that defiles, or causes an abomination or a lie, but only those who are written in the Lamb's Book of Life."* Which of these is now difficult for you to believe?

1ST MAN: *(still gazing at him with wonder)* You were a teacher to many teachers, a Pastor to pastors, an overseer to many churches, a well-known face on local and satellite televisions. You were…

NICHOLAS: Enough of useless accolades now, my brother. Whatever I have done for the Lord or being before people at that time is of no use now. We are now partners in Tribulation. *(He offers his hand in a quiet handshake shaking his hand)* I am Davies. I never expected to see you around, sir.

NICHOLAS: And that was why I was trying to hide my face from you. As a tele-evangelist and a well-known minister of the gospel, I knew I must be prepared to give explanations to many people for missing the Glorious Rapture.

DAVIES: What happened, sir? *(Nicholas walks closer to him, holds his hand, and leads him back to his corner. They both sit down, and he begins to talk)*

NICHOLAS: *(sorrowfully)* My secret and unconfessed sins made me miss the Rapture of the Saints. I knew I was breaking God's laws, but I never knew the Lord could come so soon! *(He pauses and wipes his eyes.)* What a wasted year of labor! I had led many to heaven but missed the Rapture myself! Because the Lord had delayed His coming, I thought He would not come for a long time! What a mistake! I made a grievous miscalculation.

DAVIES: All your children are gone with your wife?

NICHOLAS: They all vanished before my very eyes. *(FLASHBACK)*

SCENE TWO

(It all begins in Pastor Nicholas' house in the evening. Everywhere in his lovely home is very lively. His wife and three lovely children are in the kitchen helping their mother as they prepare to have their dinner. Pastor Nicholas walks into the kitchen with a newspaper and sits at the table to eat. Plates are arranged before him, and his wife serves the food. The children settle down and the whole family begins to eat, talking and laughing. He takes away his eyes from the table a second, to look in the direction of the cooker, then he looks back at the table to see that his wife and children have all vanished. He pauses dreamily for a moment; drops his cutleries with a shock, and springs up on his feet in utter astonishment.)

NICHOLAS: What...was...where is everybody? What...is...Deborah! Eliza! *(then, he pushes back the chair and stands scanning around with disbelief.)* Moses! Beatrice! Oh! My God! What is going on....? *(He leaves the table and rushes through the passage to the living room. The television is still on. Then he dashes up the stairs calling loudly)* What is going on? Honey! Deborah! Moses! *(then he rushes* *out of the house and calls on the gateman)* Sunday! Sunday! *(A man rushes out of the gatehouse in a singlet top over loose trousers.)'*

SUNDAY: Yes, sir. I am here.

NICHOLAS: *(stammers in amazement)* Did you see Mummy and the children going out of here or …somebody…coming inside to….

SUNDAY: No, sir. Everybody is inside. I heard their voices talking and laughing in the kitchen a few minutes ago. I heard Mummy talking to Moses. They are all inside the kitchen, sir.

NICHOLAS: *(then, he screams)* No-o-o-o! It mustn't be! *(He rushes inside the house again, the gateman still stands, wondering. He rushes up the stairs and begins to open the door of the rooms one after the other only to reveal emptiness with untidy rooms. Then he screams very madly and storms into his room.)* What has happened to me? It mustn't be! My wife …and my three children…vanishing just in a second right before me…! I hope it is not….? *(Then, he grabs his cell phone and calls a number. Inside a large bungalow, the phone is ringing on a stool beside a long settee in the living room. A newspaper, a pair of eyeglasses, and house slippers lay in front of the settees. The cell phone keeps ringing until a woman walks into the living room briskly and picks up the phone.)*

WOMAN: *(lively)* Hello…Rev. Nick, evening…how is it…?

How is Sister Debby and the ...?

NICHOLAS: *(hastily cuts in)* Is your husband there...? Is Deacon Edwards there?

SIS. DEBBY: He is not here, but he must be in the room upstairs. What is the problem, Rev.?

NICHOLAS: No...no problem.... where are your children?
(A young lady comes down the stairs into the living room)

SIS. DEBBY: *(becoming worried)* They are all here...this is Veronica here...the younger ones are in the room...what is the problem, Sir?

NICHOLAS: *(sweating apprehensively)* Get your husband on the phone for me...please.

SIS. DEBBY: *(to Veronica)* Take the phone to your father in the room, Pastor wants to speak with him.

VERONICA: Just coming from his room, I left him down here reading the newspapers. He is not in his room...

SIS. DEBBY: *(speaking to the receiver)* Vero said he is not in the room; we will check outside for him. But can't you discuss the matter with me...?

NICHOLAS: He is not in his room, and he is not found where your daughter left him...what about your children...? Tolu...Bisi...? Check the rooms for them.

SIS. DEBBY: *(to Veronica)* Are Tolu and Bisi in the room?

VERONICA: *(anxiously)* I thought they were with you in the kitchen!

SIS. DEBBY: What! *(She leaves Veronica and rushes up to the room. Madly, she begins to open all the rooms and then the toilet and bathroom. Then she screams aloud on the phone)* Reverend, ...! I can't find my children...what has happened...My God...!

NICHOLAS: *(shaking in tears)* I don't know, Deaconess. Let me confirm. I will call you back. (*He cuts the call and rushes back to the living room and looks at the television which now beams BREAKING NEWS. Then, the news is broadcast:*
"The time is 5:00 pm.
Here is the news in brief.
There has been a commotion since a couple of minutes ago throughout the four corners of the federation due to the sudden disappearance of some groups of people. The people concerned have reportedly vanished suddenly from their various places of work, homes, and from the streets and from inside cars and taxicabs. It was reported that the sudden disappearance took place within a twinkling of an eye and the cause of the incident is yet to be known.
There was a plane crash a few hours ago at the Kenyan-Tanzanian border. The cause of the crash according to keen investigation was due to the sudden disappearance

of the pilot and the co-pilot from inside the cockpit. The plane lost control and crashed on top of a mountain at the border with more than 150 passengers burnt beyond recognition.

Many hospitals are filled with accident victims who are both injured and dead because of multiple accidents on the roads and highways.

The Central Command, of the nation's police force is now packed full of hundreds of frightened people who had come to report the missing of their babies and children including relatives and loved ones.

Reports from our International Correspondents from Europe, America, Asia, and many nations of Africa have confirmed that the situation is now believed to be similar throughout the whole world, and it has been reported emphatically that the majority of these missing ones, if not all of them are known to be mostly believers of the Biblical Jesus Christ. Stay tuned for more news at 7:00.

Thank you.

> *(He stands glued to the spot and gazing at the television screen, long after the news is signed off. Then he screams, falls on the couch, and bursts into tears.)*

NICHOLAS: *(weeping bitterly)* Oh…no-o-o-o! I have missed it! I have missed the glorious Rapture! Oh…. I have missed the glorious hope of all ages…. Ah…! I am finished…! Ah…! Deborah…! Moses! Eliza…Beatrice…Ah! My wife…my children. They are all gone….! Ah! I missed the glorious hope of the Saints…Ah…I am finished…

> *(His phone rings again and he picks it up quickly. It is Deaconess Edwards, in tears, her daughter*

sobbing on the floor beside her)

SIS. DEBBY: *(tearfully)* Pastor, have you heard? It was the Rapture…

NICHOLAS: *(sobbing uncontrollably)* Yes, …we just missed it! We missed the glorious hope of all Saints… *(then, he cuts the call and throws the phone on the floor before him and wails in regret. It has been a FLASHBACK.)*

SCENE THREE

(Back from the Flashback, they are both sitting down beside each other, the ray of the shining moonlight brightens their sorrowful faces. Nicholas' face is drenched in sorrowful tears as he finishes narrating the flashback to his newfound friend.)

NICHOLAS: And so, with my eyes opened, that was how I missed the Great Surprise the Lord had reserved for all those who had looked forward to his glorious appearance. I wonder what is going on up there now. My wife and my children will not find me beside them. I missed the glorious gathering of all Saints of the ages in the Cloud. I missed the glamorous Marriage Feast of the Lamb, where angels shall serve and produce inexplicable sonorous music; I missed the beautiful sights of the Heavenly environment and the breathtaking parade of the ancient Saints in dazzling white robes. The reward of the Saints with crowns, ceremonies, heavenly anthems, and melodies and …. Oh! My God…!

DAVIES: *(looking at him with surprise)* I was born in a Christian home. My parents are devoted Christians, but all my life I have avoided Christian living. I have been obstinate and disobedient to the ways of God. On many occasions, I have heard my father talked about the coming of Jesus Christ, but I have never given it a thought. On the Rapture Day, I was with my girlfriend, a choir leader of a Pentecostal church.

SCENE FOUR

(Inside a moderate size room. A lady lies on the bed, the large cloth covering her up to her chest. Davies comes out of the bathroom, in an underwear singlet, belting up his trousers. He notices the lady looking sad.)

DAVIES: *(sitting down to wear his shoes)* Baby, what's up? Why are you looking sad?

THE LADY: Each time you come to visit, you always make me do what I don't want to do.

DAVIES: Since we agreed we shall get married, there is nothing to be sad about. We are already in love together. What about all those couples who have one or two children before they go to the altar?

THE LADY: A child of God is not supposed to do this before marriage. I don't always feel good about this.

DAVIES: *(playfully moves closer to her) Look* at me, Mercy, just look at me. Are you going to marry me?

MERCY: *(Rising halfway)* Yes, Pelu. But this is a sin. Let's stop doing this. Since we started this relationship, my spiritual life has not been as it used to be. I resisted you for a long time until you pushed me to do what I never intended.

DAVIES: *(laughing, as he buttons his shirt)* And ever since then, I have not stopped loving you, Sweetie.

MERCY: We must stop this…
   (Then, suddenly, they hear a loud shout from an elderly woman in the house:)

GRANDMA: Who carried the baby from the sitting room? I left the baby here….! Who carried her?
   (The worrisome shooting continues. Davies and Mercy exchange glances)

MERCY: She said someone carried the baby away.
   (Outside, the elderly woman continues to shout madly in front of the house. A young woman nervously rushes around in tears; she searches places and rooms madly, crying. The elderly grandma continues shouting.)

GRANDMA: *(fretfully)* I laid the baby here when I finished bathing her! Her mother was in the kitchen preparing her milk. I went into the room to bring her clothes and I came out and discovered she was missing within a short time. Who took her from here? *(She rushes to Mercy's door and begins to bang it.)* Mercy! Mercy! Did you carry the baby from the living room? I am looking for the baby…! Mercy!

(Mercy comes out of the bathroom into the room, buttoning up her blouse. Davies had finished dressing. They open the door of the room and come out to the nervous rowdiness in the house. Then, they begin to hear other noises within the compound. A man comes down from one of the flats upstairs wondering)

THE MAN: Mercy! What is happening? What is happening?

MERCY: Uncle Seye, what happened?

UNCLE SEYE: Mosun…Mosun…!

MERCY: What happened to her, Uncle? We just talked together about an hour ago when I came to your sitting room upstairs.

UNCLE SEYE: I was just talking with her when she disappeared right before my sight.

MERCY: *(alarmed)* She did what…?

UNCLE SEYE: She vanished in my sight.

MERCY: Vanished…? *(She stands glued to the spot for a moment, trying to comprehend what has just been said.)*

DAVIES: *(wonders)* You were talking…. then, she disappeared…? *(The noises continue in the house; Mercy leaves the spot and hurries outside, Davies* *trailing behind her. She sees some rowdiness accompanied with various noises outside the house. A few meters to the front of the house, a car had crushed a motorcycle and knocked off the passenger. The motorcyclist had disappeared, and the machine had run into the coming car. The passenger writhes in pain by the roadside. Mercy shouts tensely.)*

MERCY: It must not be! It must not be! *(She rushes back inside the house, Davies following behind her, and runs upstairs to the flat of the man, and sees him wondering in fear and confusion.)* Uncle…!

UNCLE SEYE: Mercy…Mercy…what is all these about? I can't understand this. We were here, I was talking with her…then…I don't even know How it happened. In a second, I couldn't see her right in my sight.

MERCY: Ah! *(Then, she calls a number on her phone, it is ringing, but is not picked up.)* Ah! My Pastor's phone is not picked up! *(She tries another phone, and the receiver talked back)* Ah! Sister Marvelous…Sister Marvelous…!

VOICE OVER: Hello…! Mercy…! How is it?

MERCY: Where are you?

VOICE OVER: I came to the market to buy some things. But there is a riot in the market. There is a commotion everywhere…

MERCY: *(trying to control her tears)* Listen to me…It is not a riot o. It is not a riot o. It is the Rapture o. You have just missed it, so did I do. We have missed the Rapture o...

VOICE OVER: Ehn...! Rapture.... I am finished! I am finished!

UNCLE SEYE: What is Rapture...?

MERCY: Ah! I preached to your daughter...she is gone, and I am left behind! *(She rushes down the stairs in tears and dashes across to her room. Davies is still following her, at the door, she turns back to him in angrily.)* What else are you looking for? Go back! Can't you see? You ruined my life!

DAVIES: *(trying to hold her hand)* Come on, how did I... *(In a flash, in anger, she slaps his face angrily, rushes at him, and tears down his shirt. Then, places her teeth on his chest and bites him deeply. Davies screams and wrests himself free from her, wriggling with pain.)*

MERCY: *(crying with anger)* I had kept myself pure for my Lord and Master until you walked into my life, and I fell into your trap.

SCENE FIVE

(Back from the FLASHBACK. They still sit down beside each other, while Nicholas still listens to Davies's pathetic story.)

DAVIES: From her house, I rushed down to my parents' house, and just as expected, they were both gone. I think they were caught up while eating at their dining table. I could still see all the plates of unfinished food. My younger ones also could not be found. They have all gone, I have been left behind. Then all the earlier talks and messages on Salvation, Rapture, and Tribulation years; suddenly began to make meaning to me. But one of the most painful things I always remember is that I made that girl miss the Glorious Rapture.

NICHOLAS: All of us at this Tribulation time will have one or two things to regret about. How we ought to have lived our lives and what we ought to have done differently. I have misled many people. Many of my church members must have surely missed the Rapture. I was pastoring them, without leading them to heaven. I started well in ministry, but I later got corrupted along the way. Heaven no longer became my goal, but money and fame which came along with gross immorality.

SCENE Six

(Inside a lavishly furnished executive office. Rev. Dr. Nicholas is sitting behind a large office table, in a neat-fitting shirt and tie; his coat is hung over his swivel chair behind him. He talks on the phone revolving sideways, leisurely, in his chair as he speaks with someone on the phone.)

NICHOLAS: Well, my dear Pastor Herbert my honoring your invitation to bless you at your convention depends on your accepting my conditions for coming.
(At the other side, are three men sitting down around a table listening to the conversation between one of them and Rev. Nicholas.)

HERBERT: We just want to beg you, sir, to be considerate a bit on our church, sir. We really need you to come and bless us.

NICHOLAS: Well, my brother, there are some men of God you can't just call without being ready to pay some heavy price. And I am one of them. I think we will have to call off this conversation if you do not agree with my conditions.

HERBERT: Alright, sir. We shall do our best.

NICHOLAS: Good, then, let me repeat them all over again. In addition to arranging for my flight tickets and my hotel suite at the Hiltons, you will arrange for my honorarium.

HERBERT: You have told us your honorarium is N400,000 but we must pay half of it into your account before your arrival.

NICHOLAS: Yes, and I forgot to tell you that I am going to raise some special offerings before each of my sermons.

HERBERT: *(astound)* What for, sir? Apart from the normal offering time?

NICHOLAS: Divine Breakthrough Offering. I want the Lord to use your people to partake in the building of my new Pentecost Cathedral.

HERBERT: That will be too much, sir. Giving you N400,000, then, taxing our members in addition to the hotel bills and flight tickets. The burden will be too much for them.

NICHOLAS: *(smiles faintly)* Stop fretting, Pastor. Whatever offering I can raise is shared 70/30. That means, 70% comes to my building project and 30%

goes back to you.

HERBERT: No, sir. That will be overtaxing my congregation.

NICHOLAS: Alright, 60/40 then.

HERBERT: It isn't good for my congregation, sir.

NICHOLAS: Then this conversation is over, thank you. *(He cuts the conversation and a seductively dressed lady enters with a file in hand)* Yeah, Helena, cancel the preaching appointment I have with the Eternal Deliverance Missions Int'l. They can't cope with the invitation.

HELENA: Alright, sir. Just want to remind you of your preaching engagement in Enugu tomorrow evening.

NICHOLAS: Yeah, have they made adequate arrangements for my coming?

HELENA: I got their e-mail a few minutes ago. They have made two rooms ready for you and the pastor following you as your Personal Assistant at the Presidential Lake Hotels.

NICHOLAS: *(sharply in a husheu voice)* No! No one is following me tomorrow to Enugu except you. Are you not my Personal Secretary?

HELENA: *(reluctantly)* Sir, I've been feeling uncomfortable with this secret affair. I am afraid,

the church or even your wife might find out things
are going on between us.

NICHOLAS: *(smiles faintly as he draws her closer and
pats her on the back)* Leave that to me. I know how to
handle that. Nobody knows anything if you apply
wisdom. We go together tomorrow, right? *(Helena
goes out of the room. Nicholas smiles again as he
gazes at her exiting)*

SCENE SEVEN

(Back from his long thought, with sorrowful tears in his eyes.)

NICHOLAS: What a wasted year of labor! I had led many Heavens but missed the Rapture myself! Secret sins. Unconfessed sins kept me back. I regret all my actions. I never knew that... *(then, he pauses abruptly, trying to listen to an approaching footstep. He whispers)* Can you hear some footsteps?

DAVIES: *(scared)* Somebody is approaching. *(They withdraw themselves into the shadowy corner. Outside the building, they can see through the window two ladies running towards the building. He whispers in fear)* Look like...two ladies.

NICHOLAS *(staring in the direction nervously)* Look like those disguised secret police.... That is how they go about suspected hideouts to fish out those who refuse to comply with the government directives...

DAVIES: *(more scared)* See, they stop by the house.

(The ladies get to the front of the uncompleted building, and heedfully, they enter. They too look very nervous and afraid as they sneak into the house and walk to a corner of shadows.)

NICHOLAS: These are not police. They too are running. They too must be one of us, the uncompromising ones.

(The ladies hide in the shadows, looking frightened)

LADY I: *(looking distraught)* Augustina, let's go back.

AUGUSTINA: To where Betty. To where?

BETTY: *(wiping her tears)* I can't continue hiding like this. For how long shall we be running around in hunger and thirst? You can't buy anything to eat unless you have registered and given the mark on the back of your right hand or your forehead.

SCENE EIGHT

(Betty, Augustina, and another young man are watching the news on the television. They look terrified and nervous as the two ladies pace the floor about restlessly. The young man sits on the edge of the chair anxiously, glued to the news which is about to begin. Shortly, the news begins, and they all keep calm, watching anxiously.)

"The time is 2.00 O'clock.

Good afternoon, here is the World News.

Yesterday afternoon, the United Nations met in an emergency session and formed a new organization, which embraced every country in the whole world. This organization, according to the Secretary General of the United Nations, shall be called: "United Nations Emergency World Government". He further explained that it is a One-World Government designed to work for the security and welfare of every country in the world, and every government of the nations is bound to cooperate with the United Nations procedures.

The United Nations Secretary-General further stressed that this step must be taken because of the mysterious disappearance of a large percentage of the world population. The United Nations Emergency World Government Supreme Council is made up of leaders from all the major world powers and a world leader has been appointed as the President of the One-World Government. The World President shall make his first worldwide broadcast on Radio and Television, please stay tuned.

To curtail the rate of crime and lawlessness that is in the entire world now due to the mysterious disappearance, the Supreme Council of the One World Government has brought all Police Authorities and Armed Forces of every country in the world under the control of the World President.

As a result of this, every citizen in all nations has been implored to fully support the procedures and goals of this One-World government. In co-operation with the visions and goals of the United Nations, and for the benefit of everyone, the Federal Ministry of Internal Affairs has ordered that every person, male and female should report from tomorrow morning to the Local United Nations Identification Centre situated at the Divisional Police Headquarters nearest to you.

Report early to receive an identification mark in support of the World Government and the World President. The Federal Government has declared that in the interest of world security, all people who may not be willing to bear the identification mark of unity shall be treated as criminals and subjected to arrest and prolonged inconveniences and torments.

The Federal Minister of Domestic Affairs restates that the federal government wishes every citizen of this nation to know that the United Nations is taking every

step for the peace and security of everyone. Please stay
tuned for further news, information, and instructions.
I am Alex Henrimore.
 Once again, good afternoon."
    *(The three persons in the room remain sober and
    confused as the news ends)*

SCENE NINE

(The FLASHBACK ends. Augustina and Betty still stand talking cautiously)

AUGUSTINA: We have been informed that the World President appointed by the United Nations as the man of Peace, is the Antichrist prophesied in the Bible and that Identification Mark is a mark of destruction and whoever receives it will forever become an enemy of God.

BETTY: *(tearfully)* So what do we do? What else remains? We are left behind; the true believers have gone. No more hope.
   (Pastor Nicholas speaks from inside the shadows a little distance from them.)

NICHOLAS: There is hope. *(The ladies shiver in shock)* you may think you have been left behind and have no hope. But you have one hope. That only hope is Jesus.

AUGUSTINA: *(still looking in the direction of the shadows* *in shock. She whispers aloud.)* Who is that?

(Pastor Nicholas and Davies walks out of the shadows into the open before them.)

NICHOLAS: We are partners in the present Tribulation. We missed the Heavenly flight too, and we have refused to bow to the present evil system. We will not take the evil Mark.

(Augustina steps into the open, followed by Betty. Nicholas stretches out his hand to Augustina for a handshake. She keeps gazing at him without responding, while Nicholas' hand remains stretched to her.)

AUGUSTINA: *(still staring at him)* I knew you very well, sir.

DAVIES: Yes, he is Rev. (Dr.) Nicholas of God's Garrison International. He is...

AUGUSTINA: *(her eyes fixed on Nicholas)* He needs no introduction to me. I know him very well. Can you remember me, Reverend?

NICHOLAS: A lot of people I have influenced in life. I have made many make the Rapture, but I missed it myself.

AUGUSTINA: Exactly what I was about to say.

NICHOLAS: What is it?

(Augustina rushes at him and gives him two heavy slaps on the face. Nicholas staggers backward and

leans on the wall. He wonders. Augustina rushes to pick a bottle on the ground, smashes it against the wall, and charges at Nicholas with the bottle's jagged points in her hand. Davies and Betty hold her back.)

NICHOLAS: Please, Sister; why the attack?

AUGUSTINA: *(roars in anger)* Look at me closely. Don't you know me?

NICHOLAS: *(still rubbing the spot of the hot slaps on his face.)* I don't seem to remember you.

AUGUSTINA: *(still trying to rush to him and stab him)* I knew you wouldn't make the Rapture…I knew it, but I never knew I could meet with you. I have always wished in my heart, that I set my eyes on the man of God who deflated my spirit and made me lose confidence in spiritual things. You still don't recognize me?

NICHOLAS: No.

AUGUSTINA: *(still boiling)* On the 15th of July, Saturday evening, in Port-Harcourt. About ten months ago…. inside an executive suite of De Castles Hotels…Can you now remember? *(She fixes her eyes angrily on Nicholas, there is a short pause. Then she shouts aloud)* I say, can you remember?

NICHOLAS: *(guiltily)* Yes, yes. I think so…

AUGUSTINA: That was the night I lost all confidence in the Christian way and lost all respect for ministers of the gospel...I was coming from the campus; you gave me a lift beside the road and talked with me till we went into a hotel.

SCENE TEN

(Inside a hotel room. Nicholas is on the bed, wearing only an underwear singlet. The bedsheet covering up to his waist. Augustina sits beside the bed, buttoning up her blouse.)

AUGUSTINA: What about the money you talked about? *(Nicholas stretches his hand to his purse, opens it and counts some N500 notes, and gives them to her.)*

NICHOLAS: That is N10,000. Did I try? I promised you five, but that is ten.

AUGUSTINA: *(smiles)* Thanks. It will be enough for the next one week on the campus. What's your name and where do you work? Do you live here in Port-Harcourt? I would like to see you from time to time.

NICHOLAS: *(smiles)* Well, my name is Fine-Boy. I won't tell you beyond that.

AUGUSTINA: *(musing)* "Fine-Boy". What a funning name. Let me have your phone number, then.

NICHOLAS: No. I can't give you either.

AUGUSTINA: Alright, can I give you, my number? In case you want to call me.

NICHOLAS: Yes, so I can call you any time I desire to see you.

> *(Augustina leaves the bed to the dressing mirror. She sits and begins to comb her hair and making up her face. On the dressing table is a big dairy. She glances briefly at Nicholas who still sits on the bed. She opens the cover of the dairy and sees the name: Rev. Dr. Nicholas Labimtan. She expresses a shock. Then, she opens the dairy further and sees a colorful handbill of a Christian leadership seminar, with the portrait and name of Rev. Dr. Nicholas Labimtan. Then she is extremely shocked. She turns back on her seat to Nicholas.)*

AUGUSTINA: *(firmly)* I want you to tell me your name.

NICHOLAS: *(smiles faintly)* I have already told you. Why are you asking? *(She stares at him for a while, and shakes her head sadly)*

AUGUSTINA: Your name is Rev. Dr. Nicholas Labimtan, isn't it? *(Nicholas gazes at her speechlessly)* You are a Pastor, aren't you? *(He stares at her without response)* Why are you doing this? You picked me up beside the road, and talked to me like one of those wayward men from the city; you spoke various foul languages and silly slangs just to convince me you were one of them. So, you are a Pastor? What type of a man of God are you? What type of congregation do you pastor? You are a shame to your God and a disappointment to people like us. You have just compounded my problems, Pastor.

(She stands up from the dressing mirror and comes to the bed to wear her shoes. Nicholas rises from the bed shamefully, comes beside her, and tries to hold her hand in an apology. In a swift, she turns and slaps him loudly, he staggers backward.)
You dare touch me with your filthy hand? May I tell you something? As you were rounding off with me on the bed, I had begun to think that I needed to stop this prostitution and start looking for spiritual help for my life. I was trying to think of a man of God who could help me get closer to God. So, it was a man of God I was having fun with. I don't think I can ever trust any man of God or seek for any spiritual help again. You are a shame.

SCENE ELEVEN

(Back in the uncompleted building in the middle of the night. Augustina still boils in anger as Betty and Davies still holds her.)

NICHOLAS: Augustina, this is my punishment for all those wayward lives of a sinful minister of God. The Rapture I missed is my ultimate punishment. But that I did not die in my sinful life is still evidence that the door of mercy is not yet closed on me, though now, I must fight for my salvation and probably die for my faith. But I now ask you to forgive me. *(She calms down and throws the bottle away. Betty and Davies ease their holds on her. Augustina goes and sits down in a corner sorrowfully.)*

BETTY: You said that there is still hope for some of us that are left behind.

NICHOLAS: Though I lived a wayward life as a servant of God, and I am paying dearly for it, but I still have the knowledge of the Word of God about this time.

BETTY: How can we survive these harsh conditions? If you don't register and have the Mark, then you will starve to death. And if you are captured now, you either bow to the government's wish or you are labelled a criminal and tortured to death.

DAVIES: I do not have much knowledge about this period, but I am aware that there is something evil about registering and taking the Mark. On some few occasions, I had heard my father talked about it. And my friend, Maurice, a member of the Prayer Team of a Pentecostal church, who also missed the Rapture told me a lot about what he had heard his pastor said concerning this period. So, I made up my mind, I would not take the Mark.

SCENE TWELVE

(A FLASHBACK. It is evening, inside Davies's house. The living room is dimly lit with just one bulb switched on. He stands by the window nervously peeping outside through the parted curtains. The television is on. He goes to the fridge and opens it. Nothing is inside except some bottles of water. Then, on the television comes: UNEWOG – IMPORTANT ANNOUNCEMENT. He rushes to the seat and increases the volume a bit to listen to the news.)

"Attention please!   Attention please! Here is an important announcement from the National Patrol Unit of The United Nations Emergency World Government. We are hereby warning you of the danger of not receiving the Mark of Unity. No one whosoever, must transact business with anyone who does not bear the Mark on his forehead or the back of his right hand! It is very important! Report your neighbors who refuse to bear the mark of Unity to your Local Patrol Unit! Report your neighbors! Be a good citizen! Obey simple instructions! Thank you."

(Then, there is a silent knock on the door. The knocks come repeatedly. Davies stands cautiously at first, then, he speaks to the door and puts his ears to

the door.)

DAVIES: *(whispers)* Who is that?

THE VOICE: *(whispers back)* It's me. Open the door quickly.

DAVIES: Ah. Maurice... *(he quickly unlocks the door, and a young man storms inside with a small black nylon bag)* You got something?

MAURICE: *(talking hastily)* Everywhere is full of UNEWOG Police, both in uniforms and in mufti. They are arresting those without the Mark of Unity. I saw them hurling people into their vans and taking them to unknown places to be tortured or forced to receive the Mark...

DAVIES: *(desperately)* I am starving.

MAURICE: *(opening the nylon bag)* I managed to get one loaf of bread from a woman who never bothered to ask for my Mark.
(Davies snatches the bread from his hand and tears it into halves. Maurice dashes to the fridge to get a bottle of water, then there is repeated loud knockings on the door that keep them frozen with fear for a moment. Then, they throw the bread back in the nylon bag and run out through the back door. The door is burst opened and three-armed men storm into the house. They find only see the back door open.)

OFFICER 1: Go...! Go...! Go after them, they have gone

through the back door. (*The two other Police follow them with their guns in their hands.*)

SCENE THIRTEEN

BETTY: I was a member of a Pentecostal church, but I have never heard my pastor said anything about the Rapture that had just happened or about this Tribulation time of an evil World Leader.

NICHOLAS: The Rapture of the saints which we have all missed, is the beginning of seven catastrophic years of terror, war, devastating storms, earthquakes, floods, famine, diseases, and unprecedented human suffering.

AUGUSTINA: *(from her sitting position)* But all these catastrophes had started before the Rapture took place.

NICHOLAS: Yes, Augustina, we were witnesses to the Indonesian Tsunamis, the Haiti Earthquakes, the China mudslide, the Australian and Brazilian massive floods; the volcanic eruptions, the Californian and Russian wildfires; the extreme weather conditions in Europe and America. We saw all these, but we never knew they were signs of approaching greater catastrophes.

AUGUSTINA: For three days, I have not eaten. I have been running and hiding, afraid to come out in the open for fear of being caught by the Patrol Unit of the United Nations Emergency World Government. I have been under compulsory fasting. I don't know how long this will last.

NICHOLAS: This World Leader will have dominion over the world for the entire seven years. It shall be years of divine wrath upon this evil world; years of severe tribulation and persecution of those who resist the rule of the World Leader by refusing to register and receive the Mark. The Bible calls this mark, the Mark of the Beast.
(They begin to hear running feet approaching)

BETTY: Someone is coming…he is coming towards here.

DAVIES: *(rushing to the window to look)* Oh! My God!

AUGUSTINA: What is that? Who are they?
(They all move to the dark side of the corner. Suddenly, three fully armed hefty men in uniform storm inside the building and switch on their touch-light in their direction. They are bathed in bright light of the three touch-lights. They are the Patrol Unit of the United Nations Emergency World Government.)

OFFICER 1: *(aloud)* Ladies and gentlemen, you are under arrest!

AUGUSTINA: Ah! My God!

OFFICER 2: We have been monitoring your movement for quite sometimes. You are under arrest for trying to sabotage the government's noble effort.

OFFICER 3: Are you not Rev. Nicholas who used to preach on the television?

NICHOLAS: Yes.
(He lands a hard slap on his face; Nicholas staggers backward and holds his face in pain.)

OFFICER 3: It was your stubborn spirit of disobedience that made you missed the so called "Rapture" If you were not prepared to obey the laws of the New World Order, why didn't you go with the rest of your people. You are under arrest!
(The other two Officers begin to handcuff them.)

NICHOLAS: *(turning to his colleagues)* No matter what happens, never accept to take the Mark! Never you bow to this evil government! *(One of the Officers violently pushes him against the wall)*

OFFICER 2: Listen to me, Rev. Nicholas, and all of you. I was a Christian too, a Bible Teacher in a Pentecostal church, but I missed the Rapture...So, what else? No hope again. We are left behind, so, I decided to make the best use of this time, by joining the UNEWOG police. I was the one who led my colleagues here. I will fish you all out from your hiding place.

NICHOLAS:(*spits out the blood from his bruised mouth*) You are making a terrible mistake by thinking that because you missed the Rapture, you are finished, then you went for the Mark. Refusing to take the Mark of the Beast is your best choice currently, and accepting the Mark is your eternal condemnation. For receiving the Mark of the Beast, you are undone forever.

(*Officer 3 rushes at him and hits him hard in his stomach with the butt of his gun, Nicholas crumbles on the ground in pain.*)

OFFICER 3: Says who? Where did you get that theory?

NICHOLAS:(*groaning in pains*) Says the Scriptures in Revelation 14: 9-10, for receiving the Mark of the Beast, you are doomed forever. (*Speaks aloud to his friends*) No matter what happens to you, friends; do not be convinced to receive the Mark or bow to their pressure. If you have missed the Rapture and all the glories of the Marriage Feast of the Lamb, then determine never to miss Heaven. If you are not among the Raptured saints, then make up your mind to suffer and die for your faith as Tribulation saints.

OFFICER 2: Take them all into the van! (*They are all pushed out of the building into a waiting van parked nearby and driven away.*)

SCENE FOURTEEN

(A Public Announcement is going about in the city, through mega-phones mounted on top of Police vehicles. We see the cars going everywhere in the city blaring the warnings:)

"Attention please! Attention please! For quick identification and punishment of those who have refused to co-operate with relevant plans of National security, all stores, shops, and places of business are prohibited from selling or giving any services whatsoever to any customer, unless that customer bears the Mark of Unity. All shopkeepers, clerks and all employees are required to make known the identity of anyone attempting to transact business without the mark of unity. Report your neighbors! Be a good citizen! Obey simple instructions!"

SCENE SIXTEEN

(It is a dirty enclosed hall, like a warehouse. It is the place where the uncompromising ones are tortured to change their mind or to death. Tied to poles are four people: Nicholas, Davies, Betty, Augustina. Their hands are tied up to a long crossbar. There are two dead bodies on the ground; they are covered with bloody wounds and marks all over. There is a camping gas cooker burning by the side; in the fire are two long knives and a prong tucked in the flaming burner of the gas-cooker. It is apparent, they have been tortured to some extent; the two ladies are crying profusely. Nicholas and Peluola are writhing with pains. Their faces are dusty and bruised. Two Officers are standing before them, holding a long horse-tail whip. There are cries of pain coming from the adjacent torture rooms.)

OFFICER 1: Is any one ready to reconsider his or her decision? Is anyone ready to apologize to the United Nations authority and denounce that dead faith in a dead God and receive the Mark of Unity? If you do, you will be guaranteed your freedom and easy access to food, drink, and all social amenities.

OFFICER 2: And if you remain stubborn and still neglect this merciful offer of pardon, then, we have the mandate of the President of this nation, on behalf of the Honorable World President of the United Nations Emergency World Government, to offer you the fullest extent of torture.

(Officer 2 approaches the burning gas cooker and pulls out the red-hot metal. He walks towards Betty and holds her head firmly while she screams. He presses the hot metal on her forehead and removes it to reveal a portion of scorched skin turned white briefly before blood oozes to the spot. She gives a piercing cry of pain. Her head shivers in agony because her hands are tied up to the iron bar. The rest captives' trembles in horror. The Officer returns to the burner and pokes the metal back in the fire.

BETTY: *(keeps crying and shouting)* Je-e-e-e-sus! Please, deliver me-e-e! Yea-e-e-e! My head...hot iron... my head...!

OFFICER 1 : Do you wish to renounce your faith in that Jesus who has abandoned you and bow to the orders of our Honorable World President and receive the Mark of Unity?

NICHOLAS: If there is the wisest thing any sensible person should do at this time, it is never to receive the Mark you called the Mark of Unity, because it is the Mark of damnation.

*(Officer 1 raises up his long horsewhip and lands it heavily on Nicholas. He groans in pains. Then, he begins

to sing:)

On a hill far away stood an old rugged cross,
the emblem of suffering and shame.
and I love that old cross were
the dearest and best for a
world of lost sinners was slain.
Refrain:
So, I'll cherish the old rugged cross,
till my trophies at last I lay down.
I will cling to the old rugged cross,
and exchange it some day for a crown.

(While he sings, the Officers look at him disdainfully. His colleagues groan and cry.

OFFICER 2: I think we should see how deep your love is to that Jesus you claim as Lord. *(He walks to the burning gas-cooker again, and pulls out the metal, which has now turned red again. He shows Nicholas the red-hot metal and places it back on the burner.)* You have the choice of turning your back on that Jesus Christ you call Lord and walking away from here a free man with full enjoyment benefit or sticking to your senseless faith and be exposed to all imaginable torture. What do you say?

NICHOLAS: *(then in tearful pains, he begins to sing again.)*

I have heard how Christians long ago
Were brought before a tyrant's throne
And they were told that he would spare their lives
If they would renounce the name of Christ.
But one by one they chose to die

The Son of God they would not deny
Like a great angelic choir sing
I can almost hear their voices ring.

CHORUS:
I pledge allegiance to the Lamb
With all my strength
With all I am
I will seek to honor His commands
I pledge allegiance to the Lamb.

OFFICER 2: *(angrily)* So be it, then. I guess we need not waste time any longer. It is better we go straight into the actual punishment for your criminal acts. We have the mandate of the government to remove your eyes, to cut off your ears and chop off your fingers and toes till you gradually bow to a painful death. *(He goes to the burning gas again and brings out the hot metal.)* Rev. We are sorry, you will have to lose your sight first. *(The others begin to tremble in fear as he walks to Nicholas. Officer 1 comes to him and holds his head firmly while Officer 2 uses the hot metal on his eyes. There is a long piercing scream of pain from Nicholas as the others begin to shiver. His left eyeball is gorged out in a stream of blood. The others are beginning to cry in fear)*

NICHOLAS: *(screaming)* Ye-e-e-e-e-eh! My Lord Je-e-e-e-e-s-s-us!

OFFICER 1: We can still spare your other eye and carry you to the hospital right now where you will be treated and given a great relief from your pains if

you can still have a change of mind and renounce
your Jesus Christ.

NICHOLAS: *(in pains, he begins to sing again)*
Jesus is the sweetest Name I know-ow,
Jesus is the sweetest name I know.
He is always just the same, ...
Oh, praise His Holy name!
That is the reason why I love Him so-o-o!
Jesus is the sweetest name I know
I have denied Him once, and I missed His
glorious Rapture, this is my only chance to gain
what I once lost.... I love Him. I won't deny Him....He
is my Lord....and Master...
*(He takes the hot metal from the burner and
approaches Augustina. He holds her head firmly and
presses the metal on her forehead. She screams)*

AUGUSTINA: Ye-e-e-e-eh! My head! My head!
*(Officer 2 goes to the burner, brings out the hot
prong and walks towards Betty again. He tries to
hold her head to the pole, she cries aloud again.)*

AUGUSTINA: Wa-a-a-it! Plea-a-a-se wait! *(the Officer
pauses briefly, holding the red-hot metal few inches
away from her eyes.)* Please, wait...please
wait...You want to remove my eyes too?

OFFICER 2: That is the instruction we received from the
authority. You people are wasting our time; we need
to go after other criminals like you.

AUGUSTINA: *(pleading in tears)* No-o-o-o! No. Please

waits! I can't bear this pain any longer. I renounce my faith in .... Jesus! I renounce my faith in....Jesus! I pledge my allegiance to the authority...of the World President....I will receive the Mark of Unity... *(The Officers smile and return the knife and metals back to the burner.)*

NICHOLAS: *(crying in pains)* Augustina, why? Why-y? Why did you do it? Whatever the suffering and tortures now can never be compared to the weight of glory stored up in Heaven for those who hold on to their faith...Why? Why...?

AUGUSTINA: *(to the Officers)* Please...let me go. Set me free.... I renounce the faith and I will take the Mark and serve the United Nations.
(Officer 1 goes to her and loose the ropes that tied her hands up to the crossbar. All the ropes tying her to the pole are loosed.)

OFFICER 1: You have made the right choice and you have to say these words after me while you raise up your right hand in total allegiance. Then you will be taken to the Registration Centre where you will receive the Mark. *(Augustina raises up her right hand in tears, and the left hand is placed on her chest, her forehead still bleeds)*

NICHOLAS: Augustina, please, don't do this. Do not renounce the Lord Jesus Christ and do not receive the Mark.

OFFICER 2: Rev. Nicholas, do not mislead this lady!

NICHOLAS: *(continues talking aloud)* If you do, you will be spending your eternity in Hell with Satan, the Antichrist and all his demons....

OFFICER 1: I think we must silence this man once and for all. He is confusing those who want to decide and bow to the authority of the Nations. *(Augustina begins to lower her hand in confusion and fear.)*

NICHOLAS: Once you receive this Mark, there is no going back. Your future is sealed together with Satan for eternity.

(She lowers both hands in fear and begins to cry.

OFFICER 2: *(irritably)* I do not have time for all this blabbering. The man is complicating issues, let him go and stop wasting our time... *(he carries his gun and aim at him at close range.)* Die and let sensible people make the right decision!

NICHOLAS: Better. Death to me is a beautiful passage to a glorious eternity.

OFFICER 2: Then you will pass through that passage.

NICHOLAS: Revelation Chapter 7, verses 13 and 14 says: *"Then one of the elders answered, saying to me, "Who are these arrayed in white robes, and where did they come from?" And I said to him, "Sir, you know." So, he said to me, "These are the ones who come out of the great tribulation and washed their robes and made them white in the blood of the Lamb.*

OFFICER 2: *(indignantly)* Then go there and wear your robe! *(He pulls the trigger and there is a sharp loud sound accompanying the three shots.*

NICHOLAS: *(grunts his words faintly)* Thank you, Jesus! *(Nicholas' body trembles in death as he throws his head forward. Betty and Davis burst into tears more. Augustina, in fear, raises her hand in allegiance again.)*

OFFICER 1: Say this after me: "I renounce my faith in Jesus Christ...I renounce His Lordship...

AUGUSTINA: "I renounce my faith in Jesus Christ...I renounce His Lordship...

OFFICER 1:... and accept the lordship of our honorable World President as the Alpha and Omega...

AUGUSTINA: and accept the lordship of our honorable World President as the Alpha and Omega...

OFFICER 1:...the lover of mankind....and the savior of the World..."

AUGUSTINA: ...the lover of mankind....and the savior of the World..."

(Two young men in black suits and dark glasses walk in and stand in front of her)

OFFICER 2: You can now go with the security operatives who will take you to the Registration Centre to receive the Mark of Unity. *(The two men walk her out of the place)*

OFFICER 1: Shall we now proceed to the next round of torture or is anyone prepared to renounce the Lordship of that Jesus? *(He brings out the hot metal from the burner and approaches Betty. He holds her head to the pole and deeps the hot metal into the socket of her eyes. She raises a scream)*

THE END

THE AFTERWORDS....

The tortures and agonies to be suffered by those who decide to love Jesus Christ after the Rapture will be so unimaginable. If you look so well around us, don't you think the sound of the Trumpet could blast any moment from now and herald the arrival of the much-anticipated government of the Anti-Christ?

So many signs around us are preparing the way for the horrible years of lawlessness and unprecedented atrocities of an evil world government coming ahead. Youths are becoming lawless and ungovernable. Homes and marriage institutions are breaking up. Divorces are becoming rampant, even in the church of God. Holiness and righteousness are becoming more and more unpopular among most Christians.

Terrorism is incapacitating many world governments, and destructive natural disasters, like earthquakes, tornadoes, tsunamis, hurricanes, floods, and draughts are crumbling the economies of many countries.

Sexual immoralities are becoming very acceptable

among the youths and some countries are beginning to give equal rights to gay marriages in the society. The ages that invited the flood of Noah and the eras of the gross ungodliness of Sodom and Gomorrah have come upon us.

All these and more are indications that the Rapture of the Saints could very soon give way to the evil government of the Anti-Christ.

To miss the Rapture is the worst nightmare that could happen to any child of God and a minister of the Gospel. Yet, unconfessed sins, unrighteousness, and unholy living will surely make any child of God miss the Rapture and spend years of agony afterward.

This drama piece is written and **shot** into a movie to help people adjust their lives and live a life that will not count them worthy of the…The Tribulation Night.

Section Two

In the Shadow of Chaos

A Poetic Embrace of

Mike Bamiloye's

"Tribulation Night" Play

Introduction

Welcome, dear reader, to a poetic voyage that delves into the heart of chaos and the unyielding agony that awaits those left behind after the saints are called home. "In the Shadow of Chaos" is a soul-stirring anthology, a poignant companion to the enthralling play "Tribulation Night," authored by the visionary Evang. Mike Bamiloye.

Within the verses of this anthology, you shall embark on an evocative odyssey, traversing the landscape of a world engulfed in turmoil and despair. The rapture of the saints, a celestial event of cataclysmic proportions, is the fulcrum on which this poetic journey balances. As you delve into these poetic narratives, brace yourself for a profound exploration of human emotions and experiences amid a world shattered by divine decree.

While "In the Shadow of Chaos" bears poetic allure and artistic charm, it also sounds an urgent warning that the rapture looms on the horizon. It stands as a poignant reminder that the celestial trumpet may sound at any moment, and the time for preparation is now. The tribulations portrayed in these verses mirror only a little of the unyielding realities that await those who find themselves unprepared, adrift in the tumultuous seas of a world void of divine grace.

Dear reader, as you immerse yourself in the mesmerizing embroidery of words, may your heart be stirred, and your soul awakened to the pressing need for readiness. The call of the trumpet may resound with unexpected swiftness, and the opportunity for eternal redemption may vanish like the morning dew.

Let these poetic verses serve as a fervent plea to seek salvation, to draw closer to the embrace of faith, and to align our hearts with the divine purpose. The rapture is not a distant tale of fiction; it is an imminent reality that beckons humanity to prepare for the celestial journey that lies ahead.

As you read on, let your heart be moved by the unexplainable agony of those left behind after the rapture. The tribulations depicted in these verses mirror the timeless truths found in the Scriptures, reminding us that there is no greater tragedy than to be unprepared for the day of the Lord.

May the words etched upon these pages inspire deep reflection, spiritual awakening, and a resolute commitment to embrace the eternal promise of salvation. Let the stirring verses within this anthology be a catalyst for seeking divine mercy and grace, for the time is near, and the sands of the hourglass are swiftly falling.

Before we embark on this poetic sojourn, let us heed the wisdom of the Scriptures, as it is written in 1 Thessalonians 4:16-17 (NIV):

"For the Lord himself will come down from heaven, with a loud command, with the voice of the archangel and with the trumpet call of God, and the dead in Christ will rise first. After that, we who are still alive and are left will be caught up together with them in the clouds to meet the Lord in the air. And so we will be with the Lord forever."

Dear reader, as you journey through these poetic verses, may the divine message resonate within your heart, may it ignite a flame of urgency, and may it kindle the embers of faith and hope. May you find blessings in these words, and may your spirit be enriched as you walk through the pages of "In the Shadow of Chaos: A Poetic Embrace of Mike Bamiloye's "Tribulation Night" play Amen.

Olumide Oki
July 2023

BEFORE THE BEGINNING
In the Veil of Fear:
ESCAPE TO FREEDOM

In shadows cast by looming trees,
A dusty road, where fear did seize,
Two friends, pursued by armed despair,
Their hearts weighed down by fateful dare.

Davies and Maurice, fleeing fast,
Their footsteps echoing in the past,
With breaths that heave and hearts that pound,
They hoped to leave the danger's ground.

But as they ran, the chase grew near,
The lawmen's wrath was all too clear,
And glancing back, they saw the dread,
Of officers who aimed to shred.

Into a bush, they sought to hide,
With fear and courage side by side,
Yet fate would show its cruel hand,
As bullets flew and pierced the land.

A shot rang out, Maurice did fall,
In agony, he gave his all,
His body wounded, strength now gone,
He urged his friend to journey on.

"Davies, I've been hit," he said,
A whisper weak, with tears that bled,
But Davies would not leave his side,
He pulled him close, their fate to bide.

"Try more, my friend, let's disappear,
From their cruel gaze, let's persevere,"
Yet once again, the shot did ring,
Another wound, another sting.

Maurice, now faint, could only plead,
"Davies, go now, I beg, take heed,
Remember what I've said to you,
The Mark, my friend, don't dare pursue."

With tears that flowed, Davies took flight,
He left his friend, his heart alight,
In desperation, pain, and strife,
He ran to save his precious life.
Maurice, with strength he could not keep,
Laid by a tree, his wounds ran deep,
The officers, with hearts of stone,
Arrived to claim him as their own.

"You're under arrest," they claimed with pride,
But Maurice knew, he soon would bide,
His time on Earth was at its end,
But in his soul, he found a friend.

With dying breath, he smiled so faint,
"Too late," he said, his voice so quaint,
"Thanks for the shot, my dear old foes,
In heaven's arms, my spirit goes."

He clutched his side, in pain he cried,
"Thank you, Jesus," he said, eyes wide,
And as his life began to fade,
He knew his choice had not betrayed.

The officers, they shook their heads,
Their hearts unmoved, their spirits dead,
They left him there, alone to die,
To catch the other, they would try.

Through tears and sorrow, Davies ran,
 With memories of his fallen man,
He knew he'd carry Maurice's plea,
To shun the Mark, and to stay free.

SEEKING SOLACE IN THE SHADOWS

Under the shroud of moonlit night,
Davies fled with all his might,
Towards an old, unfinished dwelling,
In a remote place, shadows dwelling.

In hand, a bag of black nylon tight,
His footsteps hushed, his heart alight,
He cautiously stepped inside the place,
A wearied soul, seeking a brief embrace.

In a corner, he sought his reprieve,
With loaf in hand, he took his leave,
Exhausted, he rested his weary frame,
Beneath the moon's soft, silvery flame.

But in that building, dark and forlorn,
Another man crouched, scared and worn,
Afraid of footsteps, he hid his face,
In shadows cast, he found his space.

From the darkness, he peered out to see,
A figure there, who sought to be free,
The first man rose, prepared to flee,
But the second called, "Don't run from me!"

"I too am hiding, as you can see,
A fellow believer, just like thee,"
For days he hid within that place,
Seeking refuge from life's bitter chase.

The first man, solemnly, revealed his pain,
"My loved ones gone, and all in vain,
I missed the great event, you see,
My family gone, oh, woe is me."

He turned to face the man in shade,
And shock adorned his features displayed,
Recognizing him from the TV screen,
A reverend, wise, a godly sheen.

"Rev. Nicholas," the man exclaimed,
"I've heard your teachings, highly famed,
Your messages, so full of grace,
In Christian leadership, you have a place."
But Nicholas turned, eyes filled with shame,
Haunted by his fall from fame,
He sought to leave, to fade away,
But the first man begged him there to stay.

"Oh, don't depart, my friend of old,
Share your story, brave and bold,
What happened to you, I must know,
How did you stumble, fall so low?"

With heavy heart and soul laid bare,
Nicholas finally spoke, burdened with care,
"I strayed from my calling, lost my way,
In pride and darkness, I did sway."

"The glimmer of fame led me astray,
From humble teachings, I did sway,
Now here I hide, a broken man,
Seeking forgiveness, God's guiding hand."

Chapter 2

THE REVEREND'S REGRET

In sorrowful tones, Nicholas confides,
The Rapture came, and truth collides,
The wheat and tares, separated true,
True Christians revealed, the chosen few.

Amazed, the first man cannot believe,
As Nicholas shares, he can't conceive,
The Word of Jesus, the Book of Life,
Entrance to heaven, the path so rife.

"You were a teacher to many teachers,
A Pastor to pastors, revered preachers,
Well-known face on TVs far and wide,"
Davies exclaims, with wonder beside.

Nicholas humbly brushes praise away,
Past glories gone, his heart's dismay,
"We're partners now in tribulation,"
He says, offering a quiet handshake sensation.

With hands entwined, Davies introduces,
His name, his fate, their lives now nooses,
Nicholas, once known, now shrouds his face,
Hiding from judgment in this secret place.

A tele-evangelist, a minister grand,
His fall from grace, he cannot withstand,
Prepared to explain his absence to all,
For missing the Rapture's glorious call.

"What happened, sir?" Davies implores,
In the corner, they sit, sadness pours,
Nicholas opens up, his heart revealed,
Sins unconfessed, his fate now sealed.

"My secret sins, I knew I transgressed,
Breaking God's laws, my soul distressed,
I never thought the Lord would come so soon,
A wasted life, beneath the moon."

Years of labor, leading souls to heaven,
But missed the Rapture, unforgiven,
He miscalculated, time did delay,
Believing the Lord would not come that day.
"All your children, gone with your wife?"
Davies asks, sharing his own strife,
"They vanished, yes, before my eyes,
In the twinkling of the moonlit skies."

Regret and sorrow, Nicholas bares,
His heart weighed down by heavy cares,
His family gone, his soul in pain,
He longs to undo his sins' dark stain.

Chapter 3

THE FLASH: LOST IN THE RAPTURE

In Nicholas' house, a family thrives,
With love and laughter, their home derives.
His wife and kids, a joyful clan,
Preparing dinner, according to plan.

Nicholas, the pastor, takes his seat,
His family gathers, joyfully they meet.
Plates served before him, a meal so grand,
Talking and laughing, they take a stand.

A moment's distraction, he glances away,
And back to the table, to his dismay,
His wife and children, vanished without a trace,
A look of shock on his startled face.

"What's going on?" he cries in despair,
Calling their names, searching everywhere.
Through the house he rushes, in panic and fright,
In the kitchen, the living room, day turning to night.

The gateman, Sunday, stands in surprise,
No one left, he can't believe his eyes.
"They were all here," Nicholas cries in despair,
Invisible forces seem to be at play, it's not fair.

He dials a number, a friend he calls,
To understand this strange and eerie thrall.
Deacon Edwards' wife answers the phone,
Nicholas seeks answers, feeling so alone.

The friend's children are safe and sound,
But Nicholas' family, nowhere to be found.
Debby, the deaconess, searches high and low,
Frantic for her children, fear begins to grow.

Nicholas' heart races, a knot in his throat,
As he watches the news, a frightening report.
Commotion spread across the land,
People vanished, like grains of sand.

From work, from homes, from streets they went,
In an instant, their presence spent.
A mysterious force swept them away,
Leaving loved ones in disarray.
A plane crashed on the border's edge,
The pilots gone, the world on edge.
A mountain claimed more than a hundred lives,
Lost souls left in burning skies.

Accidents on roads and highways vast,
Left hospitals filled, a devastating blast.
In fear and grief, the people arrived,
To seek lost children, no one survived.

The Central command, with panic rife,
Brimmed with souls, seeking lost life.
Reports from afar confirmed the dread,
Across the globe, the missing ones widespread.

Mostly believers of Jesus Christ, they say,
Gone in a twinkling, on that fateful day.
The Rapture, they called it, the glorious hope,
A celestial event, where the faithful elope.

Nicholas watched, glued to the screen,
His heart shattered, his soul unclean.
He missed the moment, the glorious flight,
Regret consumed him, a painful plight.
His family, his dear ones, all now gone,
In sorrow, he wept, his spirit forlorn.
Deaconess Edwards called in tears,
Her daughter sobbing, gripped by fears.

They too had missed the Rapture's call,
Left behind, while the righteous did enthrall.
A world in chaos, darkness draped,
The faithful taken, the rest left gaped.

In sorrow, Nicholas fell on the couch,
A wretched man, his heart did vouch,
For the love he lost, the chance that passed,
In anguish, he wept, his soul harassed.

Chapter 4

Missed Rapture

In the moonlight's glow, two souls confide,
Davies and Nicholas, their hearts open wide.
Tears of sorrow glisten, their faces damp,
As Nicholas shares a tale, like a mournful camp.

His flashback unfolds, a story so dire,
A missed opportunity, a heartrending mire.
He recounts the day, the Rapture's call,
When the heavens opened, and angels did enthrall.

"My eyes were opened," Nicholas starts,
With sadness in his voice, he shares his heart.
"I missed the surprise, the glorious event,
The Lord's appearing, to all He had sent.

"My wife and children, without me there,
In the Cloud they gathered, a celestial affair.
The Marriage Feast of the Lamb so grand,
With angels serving, a heavenly band.

"Inexplicable music filled the air,
The sights so breathtaking, beyond compare.
Ancient Saints, in robes so white,
Paraded with grace, a celestial sight.

"Crowns for the Saints, ceremonies so bright,
Heavenly anthems and melodies take flight.
Oh, what have I missed, my God above,
The reward of the Saints, eternal love."

Davies listens intently, his heart stirred,
A Christian home, yet he's been deferred.
Rebellious and obstinate, he chose his way,
Ignoring the truth, despite what his parents say.

On that Rapture day, he was with his love,
A choir leader, guided by faith from above.
But he paid no heed, to the warnings so clear,
As the world unfolded, and the end drew near.

In a moderate room, sorrow fills the air,
Davies and Mercy, burdened hearts they bear.
Wrapped in a cloth, Mercy lies on the bed,
A tale of love and sin, they both have tread.
"Why are you sad?" Davies asks with care,
Their love entwined, yet shadows linger there.
"We'll soon be wed," he assures with cheer,
But Mercy's heart, conflicted and unclear.

"A child of God," she whispers, pained,
"We should abstain, our souls not stained."
She longs for a love that's pure and divine,
Yet finds herself caught with Davies in a tangled line.

Davies laughs, he doesn't seem to heed,
Love blinding judgment, his heart takes the lead.
"Since we're in love," he confidently states,
"Others have erred, before marriage, they've mated."

But deep inside, a voice of guilt and shame,

Haunts Mercy's soul, she feels the blame.
Her spirit wanes, her faith's obscured,
Their love entangled, their hearts immured.

As they converse, a shout rings through the space,
A baby missing, in the bustling place.
The elderly grandma cries in distress,
Her grandchild vanished, a heart's duress.
In the house, commotion's on the rise,
The child disappeared, to everyone's surprise.
Mercy's heart races, fear takes hold,
Uncertainty abounds, the truth unfolds.

Another woman searches, her daughter gone,
In seconds, vanished, her presence none.
The man upstairs, his voice trembling,
A loved one lost, a surreal awakening.

Mercy hears the news, her heart sinks deep,
A revelation dawns, fear's grip takes leap.
"It can't be true," she pleads in despair,
The Rapture's come, she's left unaware.

Calling her pastor, her voice trembles fast,
The truth revealed, her heart broken at last.
"We've missed the Rapture," she cries in grief,
Her soul in turmoil, seeking belief.

And Uncle Seye confused, can't comprehend,
His daughter gone, vanished without end.
Mercy's anger surges, grief takes flight,
Directed at Davies, in anguish and spite.
"Now I'm here," Davies admits with pain,
Avoiding the truth, living life in vain.
My father spoke of Christ's return,
But I closed my heart, with arrogance I spurn.

"The Rapture came, and I was left behind,
Regret fills my soul, with love I'm blind.
I wish I'd listened, to my father's voice,
Embracing the truth, making a righteous choice.

Davies shares his pain, a tragic fate,
His loved ones vanished, left to wait.
Also His parents' home, once filled with cheer,
Now empty and cold, his heart in fear.

He rushed to find them, all in vain,
The Rapture took them, in one swift chain.
Unfinished meals, a poignant sight,
His family gone, into the night.

As Davies speaks, his voice so strained,
The truth of it all, his heart's now gained.
The messages of salvation he'd ignored,
Now bear their weight, his soul's deplored.

"I've been left behind," he cries in sorrow,
Regret fills his heart, come tomorrow.
The Rapture came, and he missed the flight,
A painful truth, in the darkest night.

Nicholas, too, he bears his cross,
A pastor led astray, from righteous cause.
He once preached the Word, salvation's light,
But wealth and fame dimmed heaven's sight.

He knows his errors, his path misled,
A life of sin, his soul in dread.
He lost his way, the righteous trail,
Forsaking heaven for the world's grand hail.

In this Tribulation, a time of regret,
Both men ponder, their souls beset.
They seek redemption, a chance to mend,
Their hearts now yearning, for God to befriend.

Chapter 5

THE FLASH: FAME AND FOLLY

In a lavish office, with power and might,
Pastor Nicholas sits, his eyes shining bright.
His phone in hand, a conversation engaged,
With Pastor Herbert, a deal to be staged.

"I'll come, my friend, if you meet my need,
My conditions set, a contract we'll feed."
Pastor Herbert pleads, his voice sincere,
"We need your blessing, your presence here."

Nicholas smiles, in his swivel chair,
His demands grand, beyond compare.
Flight tickets and a suite at the Hiltons,
An honorarium too, to fulfill his wills.

Pastor Herbert gasps, his heart in despair,
A heavy burden, too much to bear.
"Our members," he pleads, "will feel the strain,
With offerings and taxes, they'll face the pain."

But Nicholas persists, his project in sight,
A Pentecost Cathedral, a divine flight.
He offers a deal, 70/30 he'll share,
With the church's offering, his dream to repair.

But Pastor Herbert pleads, his congregation's plight,
Nicholas concedes, they'll make it right.
60/40, he says, his heart in a bind,
To build his cathedral, his vision aligned.

With the conversation cut, Nicholas turns,
To Helena, a seductive fire that burns.
She enters with a file, her charm revealed,
His personal secretary, his secrets concealed.

He plans a trip, to Enugu he'll go,
To preach the word, his fame to show.
But Helena's worried, their secret affair,
Could cause a scandal, a dangerous snare.

Nicholas reassures, he's in control,
His charm and wit, a masterful role.
They'll go together, to Enugu's call,
No one will know, their secret enthrall.
As Helena leaves, Nicholas smiles again,
In his world of power, he reigns supreme.
But deep inside, a darkness grows,
His soul entangled, a heart that knows.

For in pursuit of fame and wealth,
He's lost his way, his spiritual health.
In the quest for more, he's lost the truth,
In greed and lust, his soul aloof.
Nicholas reflects, his conscience awakes,
As the night grows darker, his heart aches.
Secret sins now haunting, his soul torn,
The pursuit of earthly gains, a crown of thorns.

In the quiet of his study, he kneels to pray,

Tears of repentance, he can't delay.
He confesses his sins, his heart laid bare,
His pride and greed, the burdens he must bear.

He remembers the teachings, the warnings clear,
The rapture's promise, ever so near.
But blinded by frivolities, he strayed from grace,
In the quest for worldly ephemerals, he lost his place.

"I led many to Heaven," he mourns,
But in the Rapture, his soul was torn.
Secret sins and unconfessed wrongs,
Kept him back, his heart in throngs.

The weight of actions, heavy as lead,
He never knew the toll they'd tread.
A moment of truth, a sudden pause,
Footsteps approaching, an unknown cause.

Davies trembles, fear in his eyes,
In shadows they hide, whispers like sighs.
Two ladies approach, their steps unsure,
Nervous and afraid, hearts impure.

"These are not police," Nicholas fears,
Like them, the uncompromising adheres.
Running from oppression, hunger, and thirst,
In a world where the wicked is well-versed.

Augustina pleads, her spirit torn,
"Let's go back, Betty, no more to mourn."
But Betty knows, they can't comply,
For the mark of the beast, they can't deny.
In a world of chaos, darkness unfurls,
Where truth and righteousness face the whirls.

Nicholas regrets his prideful stride,
He sought fame and wealth, but truth denied.

Chapter 6

THE FLASH:
A GLOBAL ANNOUNCEMENT

In a world gripped by fear and plight,
Betty, Augustina, and a young man, filled with fright,
Gather 'round the TV, hearts pounding, feeling small,
As the news proclaims the rise of a grand global call.

"The time is 2.00 O'clock," the newsman's voice resounds,
A momentous announcement, uncertainty abounds,
The United Nations convened, in an urgent session,
To create an organization, unifying every nation.

They named it "United Nations Emergency World Government,"
A grand vision to unite all lands, an unprecedented event,
With a mission to safeguard, protect, and provide,
For the security and welfare, no country to be denied.

An organization, vast and grand, no borders to confine,
One-World Government, a concept, both divine and malign,
As the ladies pace restlessly, their minds do race,
How will this new order unfold, what will it embrace?

The young man, on the edge of his chair, glued in place,
Anxiously watches, wondering what challenges to face,
The Secretary General's words, they ring clear,
Every nation, compelled to cooperate, to adhere.

A vision to bridge divides, to mend the broken ties,
To address global challenges, no nation left behind,
But as dreams of unity sprout, fears also grow,
Can a world united truly withstand such a massive throw?

Questions arise, doubts ignite, a complex tapestry,
In this sea of uncertainty, what will the future be?
Will the unity sought, a beacon of hope and light,
Or will it cast shadows, dimming the world's sight?

The Secretary General spoke, his voice profound,
This step imperative, a response to astound,
A new organization, "Emergency World Government" the name,
To unite all nations, to quell fear's burning flame.

A Supreme Council formed, leaders from each land,
A President appointed, holding the world in his hand,
Awaiting his first broadcast, a message to convey,
On Radio and Television, what will he say?
To curb rampant crime, to bring law's reign,
All Police and Armed Forces, under the President's chain,
Every citizen implored, the world's goals to uphold,
Supporting the One-World Government, so bold.

The Federal Ministry, Internal Affairs decree,
A mandate for unity, a call to you and me,
Tomorrow, report to the Local Identification Center,
At the nearest Police HQ, become a world-representor.

Receive the identification mark, a symbol of unity,
In service of peace, for the world's community,
But those who resist, those who do not comply,
Shall be treated as criminals, their fate thereby.

The Federal Government, for security's sake,
Declares allegiance to the unity they make,
To bear the mark, a pledge they demand,
Else face arrest and torment at their command.

A message echoed by the Minister, unwavering and stern,
United Nations' steps, for all citizens to discern,
Peace and security, their guiding intent,
Stay tuned, further news they'll present.

In the room, confusion reigns, somber and profound,
The three watchful souls, their thoughts astound,
In this world reshaped, uncertainties abide,
How will they journey forth, with peace as their guide?

Chapter 7

DECEPTIVE SHADOWS: UNMASKING THE PAST

In a world engulfed by darkness and fear,
Augustina and Betty stand, their hearts unclear.
For they have heard a troubling tale,
Of a man of peace, but with a sinister veil.

The World President, appointed by the UN,
Believed to be the Antichrist, the evil one.
An Identification Mark, a sign of destruction,
Branding those who receive it, enemies of God's construction.

Tears well up in Betty's eyes, despair takes hold,
Left behind, their spirits waver, hope turns cold.
Pastor Nicholas emerges from the shadows near,
A beacon of hope, their faith to steer.

Shocked and shivering, the ladies stand,
Nicholas speaks with a reassuring hand,
"There is still hope, don't be dismayed,
The only hope you need is Jesus," he conveyed.

Augustina, still in shock, whispers aloud,
"Who is this man?" she wonders, feeling wowed.
Nicholas and Davies walk forth in view,
Partners in Tribulation, they have refused the evil brew.

They missed the Heavenly flight as well,
Yet unwavering in their stand, against the darkness they rebel.
No evil Mark shall they take, nor bow to the system's might,
In this time of turmoil, they hold on to the Light.

Augustina steps forward, Betty follows her lead,
Nicholas stretches his hand, offering the help they need.
She gazes at him, her memories unveiled,
"I knew you well," she speaks, her voice not veiled.

A man of God, Reverend Nicholas, stands,
Leading God's Garrison International, in faith's lands.
He needs no introduction, for Augustina knows,
Their paths have crossed before, in life's throes.

"Can you remember me, Reverend?" she inquires,
Her eyes fixed on him, the past transpires.
In the shadows of the past, a tale unfolds,
Augustina's eyes, fixed on Nicholas, she beholds.
A man of influence, many he led to the Rapture,
Yet he missed the flight, a soul captured.
Augustina feels the pain of the same plight,
The disillusionment, the darkness, the night.

Fury ignites within her, a torrent of rage,
Two heavy slaps upon his face, her outrage.
Nicholas staggers, leaning on the wall,
Her heart cries out, in anger's thrall.

A bottle smashed, jagged points in hand,
She charges at him, a dangerous stand.
Davies and Betty, struggling to restrain,
Her fiery desire, they try to detain.

"Why the attack?" Nicholas pleads for peace,
Confusion in his eyes, seeking release.
Augustina roars, "Don't you recognize me?"
The pain of the past, refusing to let be.

On that fateful eve, in De Castles Hotels' embrace,
Their paths intertwined in a darkened space.
In Port-Harcourt's suite, a moment of despair,
A night that shattered her faith beyond repair.

In the warmth of his car, he gave her a lift,
Talked with her, sharing his life's gift.
But the encounter took a twisted turn,
Leaving her soul scarred, her heart to burn.

"I knew you wouldn't make the Rapture," she cries,
Revealing wounds hidden beneath her eyes.
Confidence in the Christian way was lost,
By the minister's actions, a heavy cost.

The 15th of July, that Saturday night,
A memory that haunts her, casting a blight.
Within an executive suite, a darkness grew,
And from that moment forth, her faith withdrew.

The man who ought to be a spiritual guide,
Led her astray, her doubts amplified.
In De Castles Hotels, the betrayal took root,
And since that day, she lived in spiritual dispute.

Nicholas, guilt-ridden, memories resurface,
The pain he caused, an emotional circus.
He now remembers, the night etched in shame,
A turning point that forever changed the game.

Chapter 8

THE NIGHT AT DE CASTLES

In a hotel room, shadows cast their spell,
Nicholas lies on the bed, a tale to tell.
His under-ware singlet, bed-sheet to his waist,
Augustina beside him, their lives interlaced.

As she buttons up her blouse, she inquires,
About the money he promised, her heart desires.
Nicholas reaches for his purse, N500 notes unfold,
Ten thousand he hands her, a treasure to behold.

With a smile, she thanks him, grateful for the aid,
A week's worth of hope, the burden now swayed.
Curiosity beckons, she seeks to know more,
His name and occupation, her thoughts explore.

"My name is Fine-Boy," he says with a grin,
An amusing alias, a facade to stay within.
Inquiries linger, she wishes to keep in touch,
To see him again, to feel emotions' rush.

A phone number she asks, but he declines,
Revealing too much may draw dangerous lines.
Yet, she offers her number, hopeful and keen,
In case he desires to meet, to bridge the scene.

Nicholas sits on the bed, contemplating fate,
Their encounter tonight, a twist of a date.
In front of the mirror, Augustina sits,
Combing her hair, a reflection that fits.

On the dressing table lies a grand diary,
Its cover unfolds, a revelation to see.
The name inscribed, "Rev. Dr. Nicholas Labimtan,"
A shock runs through her, like a sudden thunderclap.

Within the pages, a colorful handbill is found,
Of a Christian seminar, knowledge profound.
Rev. Dr. Nicholas Labimtan, the man she's with,
Her heart trembles, her thoughts adrift.
She turns to face him, her eyes filled with surprise,
The pieces align, she now realizes.
A man of God, had deflated her trust,
A moment of truth, now revealed in robust.

In the room's stillness, a moment tense,
Augustina's voice, firm and intense.
She demands the truth, she needs to know,
Nicholas's identity, he can no longer bestow.

A faint smile plays upon his face,
Her questions probing, a darker space.
She stares at him, her eyes filled with sorrow,
Her heart aching, emotions hard to borrow.

"Rev. Dr. Nicholas Labimtan," she says aloud,
Her accusation fierce, like a thundercloud.
A pastor he is, a man of God, she learns,
But his actions, a betrayal, her trust he spurns.

He remains silent, unable to respond,
His deception revealed, his true self beyond.
She questions his motives, his disguised role,
A pastor living a lie, his morals took a toll.

In shame, he stands, unable to face her gaze,
A fallen shepherd, his soul trapped in a maze.
Augustina wears her shoes, ready to depart,
Her heart broken, her dreams torn apart.

Nicholas tries to apologize, to hold her hand,
In repentance, he seeks to take a stand.
But she turns swiftly, her anger at its height,
A resounding slap, his soul feels the bite.

"You dare touch me with your filthy hand?"
She cries in rage, her pain hard to withstand.
Her hopes for spiritual help, now shattered,
By the very man she thought would have mattered.

As he staggers backward, shame on his face,
He realizes the depth of his disgrace.
A woman in need, seeking guidance and grace,
He took advantage, her trust to erase.

Regret fills his heart, remorse floods his soul,
In this darkness, his spirit takes a toll.
He was meant to be a beacon of light,
But he lost his way, in the depths of the night.

Augustina leaves, her heart bruised and sore,
Her trust in men of God, a belief she'll ignore.
For she encountered a wolf in shepherd's attire,
A deception that left her soul afire.

Chapter 9

RESISTING THE MARK

In the uncompleted building's gloomy night,
Augustina's anger boils, an internal fight.
Betty and Davies tightly hold her, they do,
Nicholas speaks, seeking redemption anew.

"My punishment is just, a sinful life I led,
Missed the Rapture's grace, my soul feels dead.
Yet, the door of mercy remains ajar,
I must fight for salvation, near or far.

Forgive me, Augustina, for my past,
My sins haunt me, a shadow that will last."
Augustina's rage subsides, a bottle's thrown,
She sits in sorrow, feeling all alone.

Betty inquires, seeking hope's embrace,
Amidst harsh conditions, survival's race.
Nicholas shares, "Though wayward, I confess,
I know the Word of God, its truths impress.

In the aftermath of Rapture's mighty flight,
A world left fractured, cloaked in endless night.
Beware the Mark of the Beast, a treacherous snare,
For those remaining, heed this solemn prayer.

Once joyous souls ascended to the skies,
Leaving behind the lost, with tear-filled eyes.
The Mark, a symbol of the devil's claim,
A path to damnation, igniting hell's flame.

Its allure deceptive, promises grand,
But don't be fooled by its malevolent hand.
For in its grasp, your freedom shall be lost,
Chains of darkness, your every hope accost.

The Mark, a vile pact with wicked force,
Submitting wills to its relentless course.
Surrendering autonomy, choice and soul,
The price too high, an eternal toll.

Enslaved by its enchantments, you shall be,
In bondage to the serpent's tyranny.
Your mind, once clear, consumed by dark haze,
Your conscience numbed, lost in a daze.

With every passing day, the darkness grows,
The Mark's corruption, its evil throws.
A world united under tyrant's sway,
Freedom's last flicker, now a dimming ray.

Yet, in the shadows, hope still finds a way,
Those who resist, with courage they'll stay.
For in their hearts, a fire burns bright,
To fight the darkness, to champion the right.

Davies, with lesser knowledge of this time,
Recalls tales told, a darkness so sublime.
His father hinted at the evil plot,

The Mark's temptation, a sinister lot.

Maurice, his friend, from the Prayer Team,
Shared warnings, visions, a terrifying dream.
He vowed not to yield, the Mark he'd spurn,
In this dark era, a lesson to learn.

As shadows dance upon the crumbling walls,
The four souls huddle, their fate enthralls.
A world transformed, by chaos and despair,
They seek a path, a guiding light to bear.

United in purpose, they will stand,
Against the Mark and its malevolent hand.
Through trials and tribulations, they'll endure,
Their spirits steadfast, their vision pure.

Chapter 10

THE FLASH: IN THE VEIL OF FEAR

In the dim-lit eve, in Davies's dwelling space,
He stood by the window, fear etched on his face.
Nervously peeping through parted curtains wide,
A world transformed, where darkness did reside.

The television played, a flicker in the night,
A message broadcast, a warning of great might.
UNEWOG's voice, a chilling, solemn call,
The Mark of Unity, demanded from all.

A Mark on forehead or the right hand's back,
The world now governed by a tyrant's attack.
No business, no exchange without the sign,
A choice to make, a fate to intertwine.

The fridge's empty shelves, a stark display,
No food within, the end of brighter days.
Water's all that's left, a scarce resource,
In this new world order, a cruel discourse.

The voice on the screen commands obedience,
Report those who defy, with no pretense.
Neighbours turned spies, betrayal's bitter taste,
In this dystopian world, freedom laid to waste.

A silent knock upon Davies's door,
In shadows lurking, uncertainty's core.
He listens carefully, his heart's a drum,
As danger draws near, his courage is numb.

With caution, he approaches, silently,
Each step a whisper, a trembling plea.
The knocks persist, a haunting sound,
In the dark, truths and secrets are found.

Who's on the other side, he cannot tell,
Friend or foe, heaven or hell?
The choice before him, a life-altering twist,
A chance to resist or be forever amiss.

The world outside, a battleground,
Where choices made, one's destiny's crowned.
To bear the Mark, to bow to the oppressor,
Or stand firm, as a freedom possessor.
In shadows cast by darkness' grim embrace,
A whispered voice breaks through the silent space.
"Davies, open the door, it's me," it calls,
A friend named Maurice, a beacon in these falls.

With haste, the door unlocks its guarded hold,
Young Maurice storms inside, tales to be told.
A small black bag, a secret it conceals,
Within its grasp, the truth of how hope reels.

"Everywhere's infested, UNEWOG's domain,
Police in uniform and mufti reign.
They hunt the markless souls with ruthless might,
Dragging them to the depths of endless night."

Desperation grips Davies's weary heart,
Starving and fearing, worlds torn apart.
But Maurice, quick-thinking, bread does bring,
A loaf of sustenance, a simple thing.

Yet fear descends, loud knockings at the door,
They freeze, their spirits shaken to the core.
Hastily, the bread discarded, they flee,
Through the back door, from darkness they break free.

The pounding hearts resound like thunder's call,
As armed men enter, searching through the hall.
But Maurice and Davies, shadows in flight,
Their spirits soar, resistance to ignite.

Through alleys dim, they navigate the night,
Their spirits bound, their will to seek the light.
A race against the darkness, hearts afire,
To escape the clutches of a world so dire.

With every step, the hunger in them burns,
Yet hope ignites, each twist and turn.
They know the risks, the danger that they face,
But freedom's worth the trials they must embrace.

Chapter 11

TRIBULATIONS UNVEILED

In the aftermath of the Rapture's flight,
A world plunged into a darkened night.
Betty, a Pentecostal church's embrace,
Unaware of the horrors about to take place.

Nicholas, with knowledge of the Rapture's sign,
Foresees a time of terror, fear, and decline.
Seven years of catastrophe and despair,
An evil World Leader's reign, beyond compare.

Augustina, bewildered, from her seat,
The signs were there, catastrophes did meet.
Tsunamis, earthquakes, floods, and fires,
All foreshadowed darker days and dire.

They speak of the Patrol Unit, eyes of dread,
An emergency government, all in red.
A world enslaved, where freedom's denied,
For those without the Mark, they'll deride.

Three days without food, Augustina stays,
Running, hiding, in fear's dark maze.
Compelled to fast, unsure of her fate,
A world of suffering, of hunger and hate.

The World Leader's dominion, a wicked sway,
Divine wrath descends, a price to pay.
Tribulation and persecution's might,
For those who resist, and refuse to comply.

The Mark of the Beast, a dreadful name,
A symbol of bondage, of shackled shame.
Refuse it, resist it, brave hearts stand tall,
In the face of darkness, united they'll call.

Footsteps approach, fear grips their hearts,
Outside the window, darkness departs.
Davies, in shock, his voice betrays,
Witnessing a scene that drowns hope's rays.

A horde of figures, ominous and grim,
Approaching fast, their chances are slim.
Who are they, what do they seek?
In this apocalyptic world, all are meek.
In shadows dark, they huddled tight,
Fearing for their lives in the dead of night.
Three armed men, their touch-lights ablaze,
Patrol Unit's wrath, an ominous haze.

Augustina gasps, "My God, what's this?"
Their hopes, their dreams, now amiss.
Charged with sabotage, their fate's sealed,
In this world enslaved, where darkness wielded.

Officer 3's voice, dripping with disdain,
Mocking Nicholas, who dared to abstain.
"You missed the Rapture, what a shame,
Now bow to our rule, it's all the same."

A slap lands hard, on Nicholas's face,

His spirit unyielding, they'll not erase.
"Never take the Mark," he boldly cries,
A testament of faith, defying the lies.

Officer 2, once a Bible Teacher true,
Now a pawn of darkness, nothing to construe.
He led the charge, betraying his past,
Choosing the Mark, surrendering fast.

But Nicholas, bruised, bloodied, and sore,
Stands firm in his faith, a lion's roar.
Refusing the Mark, despite the pain,
In Scripture's truth, his strength does gain.

Revelation's verses, clear as the day,
Warnings of the Mark's eternal dismay.
He urges his friends, his voice a plea,
"Do not be swayed, stay strong, stay free."

For those who missed the Rapture's grace,
In this Tribulation, their hearts embrace.
Heaven's glories, they may never see,
But faith will guide them, forever be.

Officer 3 scoffs, dismissive and grim,
His heart encased in darkness's brim.
But Nicholas, defiant, stands tall,
In Truth's embrace, he'll never fall.

The van awaits, a vehicle of fate,
To carry them through a world filled with hate.
Away they're driven, their path unsure,
Will faith will guide them? Will they remain secure?

Chapter 12

THE DARK DECREE

In the city's heart, a chilling sound,
The warning spreads, far and around.
Mega-phones blare, atop Police's might,
A public announcement, a mark of fright.

"Attention please!" the voices call,
A decree of darkness, engulfing all.
The Mark of Unity, a dreadful name,
To bear or not, the world's cruel game.

All stores and shops, their doors now sealed,
To those without the mark, they'll yield.
No services rendered, no kindness shown,
A world divided, humanity dethroned.

Shopkeepers, clerks, and employees too,
In fear's embrace, their choices few.
Required to disclose, to betray, to tell,
The markless souls, where shadows dwell.

Neighbors pitted against their own,
As loyalty's thread, forever undone.
A desperate plea, "Obey and report,"
To secure one's life, a deadly consort.

In a dimly lit room, fear takes its hold,
A woman restless, her fate foretold.
She watches the news, the announcement's dread,
A world enslaved, in shadows widespread.
Peeping through windows, she seeks escape,
Footsteps approach, like thunder's tape.
Her handbag clutched, her heart aflutter,
To the backdoor, she'll take cover.

But as she opens, two officers stand,
Their faces stern, a firm command.
"You're under arrest," they sternly state,
For refusing the Mark, sealing her fate.

Handcuffed and led, her freedom snatched,
A world controlled, in darkness hatched.
The Mark of Unity, a symbol of chains,
In shadows it lurks, humanity wanes.

Chapter 13

BOUND IN ANGUISH:
A HALL OF TORMENT

In a dirty, enclosed hall, like a grim warehouse's dread,
Where the defiant souls are brought to meet torment's spread,
Four figures tied to poles, hearts heavy with despair,
Nicholas, Davies, Betty, Augustina, bound in anguish's snare.

Their hands stretched upon a cross-bar, hope hanging by a thread,
As two lifeless bodies lie, marked by wounds that bled,
Beside a flaming cooker, two knives and prong ablaze,
A scene of horror, agony's haze, where pain's fire forever stays.

Tortured to some extent, they've endured relentless strife,
The ladies weep, the men writhe, embracing agony's rife,
Dusty faces, bruised and battered, their spirits deeply scarred,
In the face of terror, they stand tall, though their fate looks marred.

Two Officers stand, unyielding, their faces stern and grave,
Holding horse-tail whips, instruments of torment they wield and
crave,
Before these souls, unbroken, they present a ruthless choice,
Apologize and submit, or embrace freedom's long-lost voice.

"Reconsider your decisions," Officer One demands,
Denounce your faith, embrace the mark, and lift the bloodied hands,
The United Nations' mercy awaits, access to comforts and ease,

A life of submission, but at least, it grants a chance for peace.

"And if you choose defiance, if you still dare to stand tall,
Know the President's decree, as the United Nations' pall,
The World Government's authority, on behalf of the highest seat,
Torture shall be your reward, until surrender and defeat."

In that grim and haunting hall of pain,
Where anguish and torment forever reign,
Officer Two wields the fiery metal rod,
Inflicting pain with every move, oh, how odd!
Approaching Betty with the scorching heat,
Her screams of agony pierce the air's beat,
Her forehead pressed with burning dread,
Scorched skin turns white, blood flows instead.

Tied to the iron bar, she quivers in woe,
As her head shakes, her pain does grow,
The captives tremble, horror in their eyes,
Witnessing her suffering, hearing her cries.

Back to the burner, the Officer does return,
The searing metal, a tool that makes hearts churn,
Betty keeps crying, shouting for release,
"Jesus! Deliver me!" she begs for peace.

But Officer One with a voice so stern,
Asks her to renounce her faith and turn,
To embrace the Mark of Unity, they insist,
To submit to power and to desist.

Yet Nicholas stands with courage and might,
Defiant and unyielding against their plight,
He knows the Mark's a path to damnation,
A treacherous road, not a path to salvation.

The whip lands heavy on Nicholas' back,
He groans in pain, yet his spirit won't crack,
He lifts his voice in a hymn of faith,
Singing with strength, despite the wraith.

"On a hill far away stood an old rugged cross,
The emblem of suffering and shame's dark gloss,
I love that old cross, where the dearest and best,
For lost sinners, bared the world's heavy chest."

The Officers look on with disdain and scorn,
While Nicholas sings, his heart remains reborn,
His colleagues groan, their spirits weak,
In the depths of darkness, they all seek.

Chapter 14

IN THE CLUTCHES OF AGONY

In that dark and dreadful hall of dread,
Where evil's grasp and torment spread,
Officers cruel, with hearts of stone,
Inflict pain on souls they've overthrown.

Their anger boils, no mercy to find,
For their cruel acts, no remorse in mind,
Mandate of government, a twisted decree,
To maim and scar, to destroy and see.

"We'll waste no more time," Officer Two sneers,
As fear and trembling grip their peers,
With hot metal in hand, their fate does loom,
Rev. Nicholas, the first to meet his doom.

His eyes, the windows to his soul,
Torn apart, bloodied and droll,
A scream of agony pierces the air,
As darkness descends, a life left bare.

But steadfast still, Nicholas clings to grace,
In the depths of torment, he finds his place,
A song of praise, despite the pain,
Resounding hope, his spirit won't wane.

"Jesus is the sweetest Name I know,
Always just the same, in joy and woe,
Though I've faltered once, my faith's restored,
In His love and light, I'm forever moored."

Yet Officer One, with a twisted plea,
Offers a chance, a desperate plea,
Renounce your faith, deny your Lord,
And we shall heal your pain, restore accord.

But Nicholas stands strong, in firm belief,
Preferring torment, a soul's relief,
For once he lost what he held dear,
Now he stands tall, his Savior near.

Then, the cruel metal, once again,
Finds its mark, causing searing pain,
On Augustina's forehead, a fiery brand,
Her screams echo, in that wretched land.

"My head! My head!" Augustina cries,
Innocence lost, in agony she lies,
But like the rest, her spirit holds fast,
In the face of torment, faith shall last.

In that dim and dreadful chamber's core,
Where pain and suffering forever pour,
Officer Two, with a heart so cold,
Holds a red-hot prong, a tale untold.

Approaching Betty, the metal in hand,
She cries aloud, her soul to withstand,
Augustina pleads, her voice a plea,
For mercy's grace, a chance to be free.

"Wait, oh please, wait!" she implores,
Her eyes brimmed with tears, her spirit sores,
"Must you take my sight away?
I'll renounce my faith, I'll obey."

The Officer's face contorts with a smirk,
Authority's command, a mission to work,
"You're wasting time," he coldly states,
"Others like you, we need to berate."

Augustina's tears, like rivers flow,
In desperate fear, she must let go,
"I renounce my faith in Jesus' name,
I pledge allegiance to the World President's claim."

The Officers smile, their task complete,
They return the metal, they let her retreat,
Nicholas cries out, his heart in pain,
"Augustina, why? Why this bane?"

The weight of suffering she cannot bear,
For the promised glory, she cannot declare,
The torture's grip, too much to endure,
She surrenders faith, her spirit unsure.

Augustina pleads, "Let me be free,
I'll take the Mark, I'll serve the decree."
Her hands are untied, her freedom found,
In allegiance sworn, her heart's unbound.

But Nicholas laments, "Why, oh why?
The glory of Heaven, let it not pass by,
For suffering here can't compare,
To the eternal joy that we shall share."

With tears and pain, a choice she's made,
In the face of torment, a path she's laid,
And Officer One, with words so grand,
Guides her to pledge allegiance, to take a stand.

She raises her right hand, tear-stained and weak,
Her left on her chest, her forehead does leak,
A mark of blood, a testament to the price,
Of the faith she's lost, a sacrifice.

Chapter 15

A Pledge with Death

In that hall of darkness, despair's vile den,
A battle of souls, where choices contend,
Nicholas, with conviction, stands his ground,
Beseeching Augustina, the truth to resound.

"Don't do this," he pleads, with heart sincere,
"Do not forsake Christ, do not bow in fear,"
But Officer Two, in scornful tone,
Tries to silence him, his faith to disown.

Unfazed, Nicholas speaks, his words a light,
Warning of the Mark, a pathway to night,
Eternal damnation, a fate that's sealed,
If to Satan's dominion, she will yield.

Officer One grows impatient, seeking an end,
To the blabbering preacher, he'll apprehend,
Augustina, confused, lowers her hand,
In the midst of turmoil, her heart's demand.

Nicholas persists, with fervor profound,
A plea for her soul, in the balance, unwound,
The Mark of Unity, a choice severe,
Once taken, no retreat, no second veneer.

Fear grips her heart, tears stream down her face,
In the Officer's grip, she's caught in disgrace,
"I do not have time," he utters with disdain,
To tolerate Nicholas, his words a bane.

The Officer's gun, he raises with might,
Pointed at Nicholas, the preacher's plight,
Yet with courage unwavering, he stands tall,
Embracing his fate, whatever befall.

"Death is but a passage," Nicholas imparts,
"To a glorious eternity, where love imparts,
Revelation's verses, a promise true,
Washing robes white in the Lamb's blood's hue."

Indignant and furious, the Officer cries,
"Then go wear your robe, where darkness lies!"
He pulls the trigger, a sharp resounding sound,
Three shots pierce the air, amidst fear unbound.

In that hall of sorrow, a soul ascends,
Nicholas, the preacher, his journey transcends,
With courage and faith, he faced his fate,
Choosing the light, despite torment's weight.

In that hall of sorrow, where shadows creep,
Nicholas breathes his final sleep,
"Thank you, Jesus," his faint words declare,
His trembling body, the burden he's to bear.

Betty and Davies, tears in their eyes,
Mourning the loss, amid tortured cries,
Augustina, in fear, raises her hand,
A choice she's made, a soul's demand.

The Officer's voice, demanding and stern,

A pledge to make, a faith to unlearn,
Augustina repeats, with trembling breath,
Words she utters, a pact with death.

"I renounce my faith," she begins to state,
In Jesus Christ, her heart's true mate,
The Lordship of Christ, she lets go,
To embrace another, an authority to follow.

"The Alpha and Omega," she continues to say,
A title bestowed on the World President's way,
"The lover of mankind," her words declare,
"The savior of the World," she lays her soul bare.

Two young men, in black suits so grand,
Dark glasses hiding eyes, they stand,
Her fate is sealed, the Mark awaits,
To claim her soul, to close the gates.

With security operatives, she's led away,
To the Registration Centre, where shadows sway,
And in that hall of torment's grasp,
A heart succumbs, in agony's clasp.

The hot metal, with cruel intent,
Betty's eyes, it seeks to torment,
Her screams echo, the room recoils,
In the darkness, torment's web unfurls.

A CALL TO REPENTANCE

In a world consumed by darkness and dread,
Where signs of impending doom are widespread,
The sound of the Trumpet could blast any day,
Heralding the rise of the Anti-Christ's sway.

Lawlessness and chaos grip the youth,
Marriage institutions shattered, lost to truth,
Divorces rampant, even within God's fold,
Holiness and righteousness, no longer extolled.
Terrorism strikes, governments impede,
Natural disasters, economies recede,
Earthquakes, tornadoes, hurricanes' might,
Floods and droughts, plunging nations to plight.

Sexual immorality, youth embrace,
Gay marriages seek a societal place,
Like Noah's flood and Sodom's dire fate,
Ungodliness rises, seals humanity's state.

Amidst these signs, the Rapture looms near,
A time of great judgment, we must revere,
To miss this moment, a believer's dread,
A nightmare that haunts, fills hearts with dread.

For those who stray, unconfessed of sin,
Unrighteous living, dark deeds within,
The Rapture's promise shall slip away,
A path of agony, their soul's dismay.

The call to repentance, it rings so clear,
To turn from darkness, from doubt and fear,
To embrace God's love, His grace divine,
And be lifted to glory, His light to shine.

In the face of darkness, faith must rise,
A beacon of hope, a love that defies,
For amidst turmoil, there's a chance to amend,
To seek forgiveness, and His mercy extend.

As the world hurtles toward the abyss,
The time to awaken, to embrace what is bliss,
To stand firm in faith, with hearts ablaze,
To follow His light through the darkest of days.

For the Rapture awaits, a moment sublime,
When the faithful shall rise, beyond space and time,
To join the saints, in celestial array,
In the presence of God, forever to stay.

So let us heed the call, with hearts devout,
To live with purpose, without fear or doubt,
To seek His face, His love to impart,
For in Him alone, we find hope for the heart.